P9-CSH-236

CYBERSTORM

CYBERSTORM

BY GLORIA SKURZYNSKI

Macmillan Books for Young Readers • New York

Copyright © 1995 by Gloria Skurzynski

Macmillan Books for Young Readers
An imprint of Simon & Schuster Children's Publishing Division
Simon & Schuster Macmillan
1230 Avenue of the Americas
New York, New York 10020

Text designed by Virginia Pope.
The text of this book is set in Berkeley Book.
Printed and bound in the United States of America
First edition
10   9   8   7   6   5   4   3   2   1

Library of Congress Cataloging-in-Publication Data
Skurzynski, Gloria.
        Cyberstorm / by Gloria Skurzynski. — 1st ed.
        p. cm.
        Summary: In 2015, when Darcy Kane moves to another part of
town, she discovers that the Animal Control Division is trying to take her dog
away and that the most obvious escape is into her neighbor's Virtual Reality
Rent-A-Memory machine.
        ISBN 0-02-782926-X
        [1. Virtual reality—Fiction. 2. Science fiction.]   I. Title.
PZ7.S6287Cy 1995
[Fic]—dc20   94-45722

☀ ☀ ☀

*The author thanks Brett Kroh, Mindy Bliss, and Izzie, the Maltese
terrier, for allowing their likenesses to be used on the book jacket.*

For Barbara Lalicki
*Across seven-some centuries and seventeen years,
we've traveled from Hamelin to cyberspace.*

CHAPTER ONE

E rik Nagy bolted upright in bed, his heart quivering like a drumhead. Disoriented, he tried to untangle his nightmare from the reality of his small hot bedroom.

There! He heard it again! It sounded like an old-fashioned metal garbage-can lid banging against the courtyard. *Dactyls!* They were coming to get him! They were going to stuff him into a garbage can and throw him onto the railroad tracks.

Trembling, he forced himself to cross the room and peer through the window. It was raining, but not hard. Drops beaded the windowpane; mist filled the courtyard. The living room clock, an electronic Big Ben, chimed its note five times.

No one would be out in the courtyard at five in the morning, unless it was Jax Hawking and the rest of the

1

Dactyls, who'd come over from Brickyard Road to get Erik. In the dream he'd just wakened from, the whole Dactyl Gang took turns beating him up, and then they piled onto his new skateboard and sped away. Glancing quickly along the wall next to his bed, Erik assured himself that his skateboard—his prized possession, his solar-battery-powered, electronically controlled, motorized, graphite-fiber, fluorescent green skateboard—was still there.

He rubbed the foggy pane so he could see out more clearly. Nothing moved in the courtyard except a slithery black cat playing with an old hubcap. Across the court, a window opened and a man's rough voice shouted, "Get out of there, you…," followed by a string of swear words. But it wasn't till the man threw an empty bottle out the window that the cat ran away.

Erik peeled off his T-shirt and lay sweating in the humid room as the morning light increased imperceptibly. It had been stupid to think the Dactyls would be out there stalking him—what were they going to do?—drag him out of his apartment while his parents slept in the next room? But when he woke from that nightmare with his heart pounding, anything had seemed possible. Dactyls, with their weird haircuts and black satin jackets, haunted his dreams.

It was too early to get up. Eyes closed, he reached out to lovingly stroke the new skateboard. He'd worked a whole month, dredging slimy algae from a sludged-up

drainage system behind the bowling alley, to earn that
solar-powered skateboard. No one else in the neighborhood had one. Cranked up to its highest power, it could
race along at twenty-five miles per hour.

He wished he could show it off, but the neighborhood was so tough—plagued by the Dactyls, who often
appeared noiselessly from Brickyard Road—that he was
afraid to take it outside. Most of all, he wished he could
show his skateboard to Darcy. But Darcy didn't like him
anymore.

Wiping his damp forehead with the sheet, he
replayed one more time in his head, like a computer program run backward, the last day of sixth grade: Darcy's
mother driving the Kanes' car away, with Darcy frown-
ing—no, scowling—at Erik through the rear window.
The fight; the names she called him. The reason for the
fight.

No wonder she hated him. When Jax Hawking had
come up to Erik that day to grab him by the throat and
slam him against the wall of the boys' bathroom, all Erik
could think of was saving his own skin.

Jax had thrown his black jacket over the surveillance
camera mounted on the wall, so the security guard
wouldn't detect anything on the monitor screen. "You
messed up my arm-bracer," Jax snarled to Erik, "and now
I'm gonna mess up your face."

His fist was on its way to Erik's mouth when Erik
muttered the lie. "I didn't do it. Darcy did it."

Jax stopped his fist in midflight. "I saw you do it, wormhole."

His voice quaking, Erik answered, "No, you just saw me pick it up off the floor. Darcy was the one that knocked it down and stepped on it. It was an accident."

Keeping his eyes on Jax's fist, Erik clamped his mouth shut after that. He didn't want to add to his treachery with any more lies; he already hated himself for blaming Darcy because he was scared. But Jax Hawking wouldn't do bodily harm to a girl, and Darcy was moving away from the neighborhood. In just one more hour, she'd be gone, permanently, from Grimesdale Elementary School.

"You're a liar!"

That was pretty accurate, so Erik said nothing. As he hung from Jax's fist, his mind raced with plans to protect Darcy. Dactyls didn't hurt girls—physically. That was part of the Dactyl creed. But psychological harassment of girls—yes; the nastier the better; the Dactyls piled it on until the girls crumpled into soggy tear-stained heaps of misery. So Erik would have to stick right beside Darcy for the next hour, until she was safely out of the Grimesdale neighborhood. If Jax came anywhere near her, Erik would push the closest emergency buzzer to call the school security guard—the guard always reacted fast to a buzzer alert. There was an emergency buzzer in every hall and every classroom. Unfortunately, at that particular moment, the one in the boys' bathroom was out of Erik's reach.

"Darcy's not allowed to touch my bracer!" Jax exploded. "No female can ever touch it."

"I knew that," Erik said, gasping, because Jax had twisted his shirt so hard it was cutting off his windpipe. "That's why—I picked—ouch!—it up off the floor myself."

"I can't even get it on my arm now. It's all bent. That Darcy better start watching where she puts her freakin' feet. You tell her!" Just so Erik wouldn't forget to tell her, Jax slammed him three or four more times against the wall.

For the next hour, while they were cleaning out their desks and lockers, Erik dawdled as much as possible, hoping Jax would leave. Everyone else had gone home except Erik, Jax, Darcy, and Mrs. Armani, the teacher.

"Why are you taking so long?" Darcy asked Erik. "My mother's going to be here for me real soon." It was warm in the classroom; the air-conditioning had been turned off because of the usual summer power shortage. Darcy pulled back her long brown hair and lifted it to cool her neck.

"That's why," Erik told her. "Because your mother's coming."

"What does that mean? And why is Jax still here? Is something going on?"

At the front of the classroom, the teacher had stacked her end-of-the-year gifts from students into a cardboard box. "I'm taking this out to my car," she said. "I'll be

back in just a minute. You three—hurry it up, will you?
The custodian needs to clean the room."

Jax had been pretending to wipe out his desk with a
paper towel, which was so unlike him that Mrs. Armani
should have been suspicious. As her footsteps faded, Jax
looked at Erik and Darcy, and grinned. A mean grin,
promising trouble.

Erik couldn't decide whether it would be better to
grab Darcy's hand and make a run for it, whether to
maneuver himself closer to the emergency buzzer, or
whether he could trust Mrs. Armani to get back before
Jax Hawking made his move.

"Will you tell me what's happening?" Darcy
demanded.

Erik whispered, "Jax thinks you bent his bracer."

"What's a bracer?"

"You know—one of those metal armbands the
Dactyls wear."

"Oh, that. Why does he think I broke it?" Darcy
asked, whispering because Erik had whispered.

It was one thing to lie to Jax Hawking, but it was a
whole different thing to lie to Darcy. Erik had never lied
to Darcy, not for as long as he'd known her, which was
just about his whole life. "Well...uh...," he muttered,
keeping an eye on Jax, "I was going down the aisle past
Jax's desk, and his bracer was on the edge of the desk and
I bumped it."

Darcy nodded. She knew how clumsy Erik could be.

"So when it fell on the floor I accidentally stepped on it and bent it pretty bad."

"But why does he think *I* did it?" she asked.

"Because…I'm really sorry…that's what I told him."

"You *what!*" Darcy straightened. She'd been holding a terra-cotta flowerpot containing a miniature rosebush; Mrs. Armani had given it to her that afternoon. Setting the pot on her desk, Darcy folded her arms and glared at Erik.

Erik began to explain, but even to him it sounded lame. "Look…you're moving out of here in"—he looked at his watch—"in twenty more minutes. If I can protect you from Jax for just that much longer . . ."

"*You* protect *me!*"

"Yeah. I've checked the location of every emergency buzzer, just in case. Anyway, Dactyls don't ever hit girls." But they pulverize *guys*, he added in his own head. Leaning closer to Darcy, he hushed his voice. "If Jax knew I was the one that bent his dumb bracer, he'd… um… mess me up pretty bad."

"Oh really!" Darcy said out loud. "That sounds like a great plan to me!" Lowering her lashes and then looking up at Erik again, she whispered, "Why should I take the blame for what you did?"

At his desk, Jax Hawking wadded up the paper towel he'd been using and threw it across the room; it bounced off Erik's cheek. Then Jax stood up, cracking his knuckles as he rose. His straight blond hair was cut Dactyl style: so short in the back it looked shaved; parted in the middle in front to let two long wings of hair swoop over his ears.

"Uh-oh, here he comes. Don't let it happen!" Erik prayed under his breath, squeezing his eyes shut as Jax began to move toward them. He was so sure he was going to get mauled that he couldn't even remember which wall the emergency buzzer was on.

"Hey, Jax!" Darcy called.

Although Erik's eyes were closed, he could hear the approaching assassin grunt, "Whaddya want?"

"I... I just wanted to say . . ."

Darcy hesitated, and Erik cringed, waiting for the rest of it.

"I'm real sorry about your bracer, Jax," she told him. "It was an accident. I didn't mean to do it."

Erik's eyes flew open in time to see Jax's face screw up in an expression he must have meant as a smile. "Oh, that's okay," he assured her. "Only, Darcy—guess what? It's payback time!"

Before either of them could react, Jax leaped toward Darcy's desk and slammed against it, hard! The miniature red roses she'd nurtured all year wobbled on her desk. Just an hour earlier, Mrs. Armani had lifted the pot from the windowsill and handed it to Darcy, saying, "You took such good care of this little rosebush, I want you to have it. At your new house, you can plant it in the yard so you'll always remember us."

Darcy tried to grab the pot before it fell, but Jax blocked her. The flowers toppled to the floor, and the terra-cotta planter smashed to pieces.

"Hey!" Erik yelled.

"You want to say something, wormhole?" Jax asked.

"Uh...no." Erik shook his head. "No, nothing."

With that, Jax stomped on the rosebush, mashing it into the pieces of broken crockery with his heavy boots. Then he turned and sauntered out of the classroom, calling back to Erik, "See you next year, wormhole. Or maybe sooner." A nasty hand signal escalated the threat; Dactyls were famous for throwing signs.

"My roses, my baby roses!" Darcy cried, kneeling in the dirt-strewn aisle. She picked up the sad, torn petals and crushed them against her face.

Watching her made Erik feel so awful, so inadequate, that he muttered something really stupid. "So what's the big catastrophe? They're only flowers."

That's when she really tore into him. He couldn't remember all the words she'd screamed at him, but it ended with, "And you call yourself a friend! I can't believe you just stood there and let my roses be murdered."

"What could I do?" Erik pleaded.

"You could have yelled for Mrs. Armani! You could have hit the buzzer for the guard, like you said you were going to do. You could have hit *Jax!*"

"Me! Why didn't *you* hit him?" The thought of hitting Jax made Erik's stomach cramp. Erik was not especially physical. During the past winter he'd shot up in height; now his arms and legs, joints and muscles, seemed all out of synch. Jax, on the other hand, moved like a panther.

"Because you started this whole thing, and you said you were going to take care of it!" Darcy shouted.

"I *will* take care of it. I'll buy you another rosebush," Erik began, but Darcy whirled on him, her eyes flashing.

"I wouldn't take anything from you, ever!" Her voice quavered, either from the sight of the crushed petals, or from sheer, hard-edged anger. "You're about as brave as a cockroach! A *lying* cockroach! You lied about the bracer—you didn't even care what Jax would do to *me*!"

"I did too care!"

"I'm so glad I'm moving away from here, because I don't ever want to see you or talk to you again." She'd slammed out of the classroom, leaving Erik with a broken pot and a pile of dirt.

Almost every night, the scene played itself over again in his head. Three weeks had gone by now, three weeks in which he'd been too ashamed to telephone Darcy, even though her new phone number radiated in his memory like alphanumerics flashing on a computer screen. He heard her voice, though. Each night, in his dreams, he heard her say, *You're about as brave as a ...*

Like a cockroach, Erik burrowed under the sheet. He

drifted off into another nightmare of skateboards and Dactyls and Darcy just as the rim of the sun edged the Chesapeake waters with gold. It was dawn on the second day of July, in the year 2015.

CHAPTER TWO

"**D**arcy, come into the living room and watch the president's speech," her father called.

"Oh yutz, Chip, she might talk for an hour," Darcy whispered to her dog. "Pretend you have to go outside."

"Darcy, are you coming?"

In the living room, Darcy's parents stretched out in their inflated vinyl air chairs, peering into their Crystal-Eyes 3-D goggles. One of the advantages of the Kanes' new house was a living room wall large enough to support an eight-foot-square video-vision screen. So far the novelty hadn't worn off—each evening after dinner, Jeff and Cynthia Kane put on their Crystal-Eyes to watch three-dimensional video on the wall.

"Darcy?" Jeff slid the goggles above his eyes. "Wait'll

you see the president in 3-D! She looks great!"

"Sorry, Dad. Chip needs to go out," Darcy said. "He was scratching the door."

"Well, hurry back then.... Just look at that flag!" her father exclaimed. "It's like it's waving right in our living room. Like I could touch it! Put your goggles on, Darcy."

"Darcy's not interested in the president's speech, Jeff," her mother broke in.

"She's old enough to show some interest in our nation's government, Cynthia. She'll be twelve next month...."

The discussion petered out. Both parents were too fascinated by their new big-screen, high-density, 3-D video viewing to think about much else in the evenings. They were like a couple of little kids, Darcy thought—as if this house and everything in it were a toy box they'd just opened.

"Come on, Chip," she said, snapping her fingers. The dog padded after her through the front door and down the concrete steps, his feathery tail waving like a short-masted flag on a moving dust mop. It was good that he was white—that made him easier to see in the fading evening light.

"You stay right beside me now," she told the dog as they walked along the gravel road next to the Kanes' house, which was the end unit in a row of six town houses, all connected to one another. Being on the end meant they had trees on three sides for Chip to sniff at. "We'll

just go a little way into the woods 'cause it's getting so
dark.... Chip! Stop that!"

Paying no attention to Darcy, Chip shot forward as
fast as his short legs could catapult him, yapping as he
ran. Three crows rocketed upward in an explosion of
shiny black wings. The quiet of the hot, damp evening
cracked apart—Chip's frantic barking infuriated the
crows. They cawed loudly from the branches of a pine
where they'd taken refuge.

"Shut up, Chip!" Darcy yelled over the din. She ran
after the dog until she could grab his wiry little body,
then pressed him against her chest and tried to squeeze
his muzzle closed. Chip kept barking, but now the yaps
were just *"mmmf, mmmf, mmmf"* noises, stuck in his
throat beneath his collar.

In the house attached to the Kanes' on the south side,
a sliding door opened. Darcy looked up as an old woman
appeared on her deck, twelve feet above the ground
where Darcy stood.

Wearing a long white bathrobe, with wisps of white
hair billowing around her head in the evening mist, the
old woman looked like a ghost. Darcy had never seen her
before—the Kanes had lived in their new house such a
short time that they didn't know any of the neighbors.
When the woman raised her arm, the sleeve of her white
robe hung down like a shroud. "Is that your dog?" she
asked, pointing. Her trembling voice, as ghostlike as her
appearance, frightened Darcy. She nodded quickly, then

hurried with Chip into the thick undergrowth of the woods.

Here and there in the suburbs surrounding Baltimore, patches of woodland had been allowed to stand, but the patches were rarely more than a few acres wide—just enough to keep the suburbs from becoming one continuous slab of concrete. Once during the previous week Darcy had gone all the way through their patch of woods to see what was on the other side. From the edge of the wood, she'd looked out at another housing development very much like her own, with four-story town houses connected to one another.

The suburbs. Why did her parents think they were so great? It was true that the town house in Forest Valley Estates had scads more room than their old apartment in Grimesdale—like, five times as much—but Darcy would have gone back to Grimesdale in a second if they'd let her.

"You'll start to like it out here pretty soon," her mother kept telling her. "Look at all this space! Look at all those big trees! And no car fumes."

"And no kids," Darcy had answered. Everyone in Forest Valley Estates seemed to be either old and retired, or young and childless.

"No kids means no street gangs," her father had added.

"No kids means no friends." True, there were a lot of bad kids in the old neighborhood, but there'd been lots of good kids too. Like Courtney Payne, the prettiest girl in the school. "Payne and Kane," the other kids would call out when Courtney and Darcy walked down the halls together. "Courtney is a pain, and Darcy is insane!" It was dumb stuff, just teasing; both of them were popular and had lots of friends. Like Sydna Bartolucci, whose dad worked in a specialty grocery store. Sydna would bring star fruit—Darcy's favorite—to school almost every day and share it with her.

But most of all, and always, she'd had Erik Nagy. When they were younger, they'd sit in the apartment courtyard and read books together. By fifth and sixth grades, they still read together, but not in the courtyard— other kids had started ragging them, yelling things like, "Oooooh, kiss kiss!" Or, "Hey, Nagy, make sure you show Darcy all the hot pictures!" After that began, they took turns reading together in each other's kitchens.

Now Darcy had no one. Only her dog Chip. At night in bed, she'd tell Chip how much she didn't like the new house. Actually, the house wasn't new; it had been built thirty years ago. It was just new to the Kanes. And she had to admit that Chip loved the tall trees around Forest Valley Road; Grimesdale had been nothing but concrete, brick, and asphalt. Right that moment, at her feet, Chip was sniffing roots and clumps of dirt as if each one held a personal message for him.

A mist-shrouded moon rose above the treetops. Caws from invisible crows tore at the quiet; mourning doves cooed sadly from high branches. The skin on Darcy's arms suddenly chilled; she felt as though something bad might happen. Maybe it was because of the ghostly old woman she'd seen. "Chip, do you have to check out every single tree in the whole woods?" she scolded. "That's enough!" She picked him up to carry him back toward the house. As they emerged from the trees, the sliding door on the Kanes' deck rumbled open.

"Darcy!" her father yelled loudly. "Where are you? I need you to come in right now!"

She hurried across the yard, wondering what the president could have said to upset her father so much.

"And bring that dog!" he shouted.

"What's happening?" she muttered to Chip. Her father sounded so unlike himself that Darcy's knees trembled as she went through the patio door and climbed the stairs to the living room. In her mind she quickly reviewed the past half hour, the whole day, the entire past week, trying to remember if she'd done anything wrong. Nothing! Not only had she not done anything wrong, she'd hardly done anything at all.

Chip? Chip hadn't dug up anyone's flower box or made a mess on anyone's patch of lawn. Darcy always took him into the woods when he had to go out.

At the top of the stairs, her father stood scowling, the edges of his lips pressed into deep lines. Her mother stood behind him, looking upset.

"What?" Darcy asked.

"Look at this! There's a message in our e-mail. We just noticed it a few minutes ago."

Her father pressed a remote controller to make green letters march across a two-foot-wide section of the video-vision screen. "NOTICE—to Jeffrey Kane and Cynthia Kane, 3999 Forest Valley Road. A complaint has been registered about your dog's frequent barking. The animal must be removed immediately from Forest Valley Estates."

"Barking!" Darcy cried. "He never barks! Only when he sees crows!"

The green letters continued to blink out their cold message: "This report has been registered electronically with the Baltimore County Animal Control Division. Failure to effect the removal of the offending animal within twenty-four hours will result in a $300 fine and forcible removal by Animal Control. End of message."

"*No!*" As the letters began to repeat on the screen, Darcy sprinted up the two flights of stairs to her room in the loft, clasping Chip against her as if the whole Animal Control Division were after them right that minute.

Her parents' footsteps pounded behind her on the stairs. Darcy's high bedroom-loft had only three walls, standing completely open on the front side where the stairs reached it. There was no door like her old bedroom had.

"Honey, don't cry," Cynthia begged.

"We'll figure out something," Jeff promised, but he

didn't look too confident. "Who could have reported Chip?"

"I know who it was!" Darcy wailed. "It was that old lady next door. She started to complain when I took Chip outside just now, but I wouldn't stay and listen to her."

"What old lady?" Jeff asked. "I've never even seen her. Who is she?"

"Her name's Mrs. Galloway," Cynthia answered. "She's ancient! All little and withered and pale."

"But Darcy," Jeff argued, "you saw the old lady only a few minutes ago, and the message has been sitting in our electronic mailbox since this afternoon. It was dated two P.M."

"What does it matter? We've got to do something!" Darcy cried. "Wait! I have an idea! We'll put up a scarecrow. It's the crows that make Chip go crazy—a scarecrow'll keep them away. Chip never barks at anything except crows!"

Her father scoffed. "Forget that! The Homeowners' Association wouldn't even let us put a lamppost beside the front stoop. Everything has to look the same outside these town houses. Do you think they're going to let us stick a scarecrow in the yard?"

"So then we'll have to move!" Darcy said, kneeling. "We can't give up Chip!"

Cynthia sat on the bed and tried to pull Darcy down beside her. "Oh, honey, be realistic...."

Darcy bolted upright. "I am! If we can't keep Chip here, we'll go back to our old neighborhood."

"Forget that too!" Jeff commanded. "Now let's everybody just calm down for a minute! We'll think this through rationally. Switch on the ceiling fan and get some breeze up here." Because of summertime power demands, air-conditioning had to be turned off at eight in the evening, even though the house stayed hot past midnight.

While the four arms of the fan began to stir the air, Jeff rubbed his fingers through his scalp as if it would help him think. "Look, tomorrow I don't have to go to work," he said. "The post office is closed for the long Fourth of July weekend. So, Darcy, you and I will go talk to this Mrs. Galloway."

"You mean you and me and Mom," Darcy said. "We need to go together—three against one."

Cynthia lowered her head, letting her dark hair brush her cheek. "Oh…honey… I have to fly to Paris first thing tomorrow morning. The eight A.M. flight on the Super-Transport. I'm sorry I have to leave you during a crisis, but they've given me only ten days to write an article for *European Travel*. We need the money, Darcy. Our house payments are really high now."

"It's not worth it! I hate this house!" Darcy cried. "I wish we'd never moved here."

CHAPTER THREE

Hot, sleepless, scared, Darcy kicked off her bedspread and listened to Chip breathe. His paws made little scratching noises against the sheets; he was probably dreaming of chasing crows again. It was those awful crows that had caused all the trouble. In the old neighborhood, where people and buildings and roads and cars were so tightly packed together, Darcy'd never seen any crows, and Chip hardly ever barked at anything. But this place—Forest Valley Estates, with all its trees and space —was crow heaven. And that was only one of the things wrong with it.

Back in Grimesdale, in their crowded, cramped apartment, whenever she had a problem she could run to Erik's apartment and talk about it. She wanted so much to phone Erik right now, but it was past eleven o'clock at

night, too late to make a phone call, and anyway they
hadn't spoken since their fight. And after the awful
names she'd called him, she was embarrassed to make the
first phone call and admit how much she needed his
friendship.

She stroked Chip's silky white hair, rubbed his ears,
touched his damp nose. "You're the only friend I have
left, Chip, and now they want to take you away from me.
She wants to—that nasty old woman!"

She heard footsteps on the stairs; a moment later, the
mattress sank as Darcy's mother crawled in beside her.
"Still awake?" Cynthia whispered, slipping an arm
around her daughter.

"Um-hmm." Darcy barely answered. Her nose was
stuffy from crying.

"I want to explain about my trip tomorrow," Cynthia
said. "The call came just this evening, while the president
was talking. Darcy, do you know how many people would
give anything they owned to have the job I've got?" When
Darcy didn't answer, Cynthia said, "Plenty! I can do most
of my article writing at home; I travel to wonderful cities
in lots of countries, and everything's paid for." Cynthia
squeezed Darcy's shoulder, but Darcy wouldn't turn; she
kept her back toward her mother and hugged the sleeping
dog closer to her chest. Chip gave a little grunt.

Cynthia's voice grew husky as she said, "Darcy, when
you were born, I was only nineteen. So was your
father—just two kids out of Grimesdale High School, and

we didn't own a darn thing. Nothing! I worked all day in a scuddy job while Daddy stayed home with you. Then I came home and Daddy left for work, and I put you into the baby carrier on my back, and I went to night classes. And you were so heavy, Darcy!"

"But you loved me!" Darcy said.

"Of course I loved you!"

"And I love Chip the same way! Just as much!" Darcy remembered the first time she saw him—a tiny pink nose and two bright eyes peering over the edge of her father's jacket. "Bring me back a bag of corn chips, please," she'd called out to her father when he drove away earlier that day. He'd told her he was going to the supermarket. Instead, he came home with a puppy, six weeks old. That was two years ago, back in the time when Darcy was happy.

Cynthia sighed. "No you don't, honey. You only think you love Chip as much as I love you. Some day you'll understand the difference." Darcy felt the mattress rise as her mother got up from the bed. In the darkness, Darcy reached out, but her mother had already crossed the room to the stairs.

A few minutes later, she heard her parents' voices in their room below. It was strange how people thought that as long as they were talking in another room, you couldn't hear them.

"I feel so bad—I think she's crying herself to sleep," Cynthia murmured.

"Yeah, I feel bad too," Jeff answered. "You know, I promised Darcy that I'll try to get the old lady to be reasonable. And I'll do my best. But I have to tell you, Cyn, I'm not giving up this house because of a dog, no matter how cute he is. This is our dream. We worked too hard for too many years to make it happen."

Darcy felt her insides turn cold. So that's how it was—if things got critical, she couldn't count on her parents. She put the pillow over Chip's ears and whispered, "Don't listen to them. They don't know anything about what's important. Trust me, Chip. No matter what I have to do, I'll never let you go!"

Chip wiggled out from under the pillow. Crawling on his belly, he worked his way up to Darcy's face and licked her tears.

She could tell that her father was nervous; he kept checking himself in the mirror above the fireplace. "*You* look nice, Darcy," he said.

She was okay, she supposed: her lavender Lustrasheen jumpsuit always made her seem as long and lean as a pencil. That morning her shoulder-length hair had curled exactly the right amount, for once. Her sandals were almost brand-new. Except for the deep shadows—from sleeplessness—around Darcy's eyes, someone might have thought she was dressed up for a concert.

"You look good too, Dad," she said, reluctantly, because she was still upset over what she'd overheard him say about Chip the night before. If she couldn't count on her parents, who did that leave?

"Thanks."

"Maybe I should tie a ribbon on Chip's collar," Darcy suggested, but her father said, "No, he's a guy. Let him look the part. Are you ready? It's nine o'clock—I think we better get over there."

Although Darcy's stomach hurt from fear, she picked up Chip and bravely followed her father through the front door, down the front steps, and along the sidewalk.

"I wonder what this truck's doing here," Jeff said, pointing to a van with Rent-A-Memory painted on the side panel. "It's been parked here for the past couple days."

Darcy hardly heard him as she climbed the concrete stairs to Mrs. Galloway's front door, her grip tight around Chip. "Wait, give me a minute," she said when her father reached out to ring the doorbell.

"No use putting it off, Darcy. We have to do it."

He pushed the button. The door opened, and there she stood. She was tiny—a whole head shorter than Darcy. Her skin looked like a sheet of transparent tissue paper that had been mashed into a tight ball and then unfolded. She wore a polka-dot blouse, a long cotton skirt, and Birkenstock sandals on bare feet. Her toes were knobby and crooked.

"I guess you're Mrs. Galloway," Jeff said. Darcy could tell that her father was as surprised as she was at the woman's size, or lack of it. "I'm Jeff Kane from next door and—"

"Come in." She moved out of the doorway to let him enter.

"And this is my daughter, Darcy. And this," Jeff said in a tone that sounded much too hearty and cheerful, "is the little troublemaker, our dog Chip."

Darcy scrunched halfway behind her father, embarrassed at the fakey voice he'd used just then. Mrs. Galloway stared gravely at the three of them, then said, "Troublemaker?"

"Uh…the dog, barking? Did you make a complaint about it?" Jeff asked.

The old woman looked surprised. "No, I didn't make a complaint."

She's not telling the truth, Darcy thought. She has to be the one.

"Are you the dog's owner?" a man asked as he came toward them from Mrs. Galloway's living room. He was short and compact, somewhere in his mid-twenties, with dark eyes and thick wavy hair. "I'm Daniel Gutierrez," he said. "I'm with Rent-A-Memory."

"Oh…uh…the truck outside." Jeff made the connection. "This is Darcy, and this is—"

"Yeah," Daniel said, tugging at his necktie. "I've been wanting to meet this little guy. He's caused the most interesting phenomenon."

"Our dog has? Chip?"

"Something about the frequency of his bark."

"He doesn't bark *that* often," Darcy protested.

"No, I mean the audio frequency. The sound waves." Daniel tugged at his tie again. Although he wore an immaculate white shirt and perfectly pressed slacks, Darcy thought he'd look more natural in a tank top and shorts. He had the tight-muscled build of a weight lifter.

"So *you* made the complaint?" Jeff asked.

"Complaint? Me? No," Daniel answered.

Chip began to wiggle in Darcy's arms. "If he's house-trained, you can put him down," Mrs. Galloway said.

"Thanks." Maybe she's just pretending to be nice, Darcy thought as the woman bent to pet Chip. Grown-ups could fool you. The dog leaned his head into Mrs. Galloway's hand and almost closed his eyes; the old woman seemed to know, somehow, just where Chip loved to have his ears scratched.

"Look, we got a notice last night that we have to get rid of our dog because someone complained about his barking," Jeff said to Mrs. Galloway. "We figured it was you."

"I would never do a thing like that without speaking to the owner first," she answered.

Darcy wanted to stay suspicious, but she felt the first tugs of doubt. Mrs. Galloway sounded sincere, and in the daylight, she didn't look the least bit ghostly or mean.

"Wait a minute! I think I know what might have happened," Daniel Gutierrez declared. "On my way in here yesterday, I mentioned to the security guard at the gate that I was having trouble getting my Rent-A-Memory unit to work, and it seemed to have something to do with the frequency of the dog's bark. *Audio* frequency. And it wasn't a complaint—it was just casual conversation."

"Oh dear," Mrs. Galloway murmured. "I'd better call the manager and straighten this out. I certainly don't want you to lose your dog."

Relief flooded Darcy. She took a deep, grateful breath as her dad squeezed her shoulder. All that worrying for nothing, his smile seemed to say.

"We'd really appreciate it if you'd do that," Jeff said. "Only…uh…I'm kind of confused here," he told Daniel. "What's this thing about Chip's barking?"

"Come in and sit down," Mrs. Galloway invited them, gesturing toward the living room.

As they passed through the dining area, Darcy noticed that the rooms in Mrs. Galloway's house were positioned the same as the Kanes' floor plan, only reversed. But Darcy only noticed this with half a mind, because she was still buoyed up over the way things had turned out. No more worry! Chip padded beside her along the polished wooden floor as though he'd never been in any danger at all. She smiled down at her dog. So you're safe, you little ragamuffin, she told him in her thoughts.

Then she looked around her. How outdated Mrs. Galloway's furniture looked, and how uncomfortable!

The chairs were straight-backed, made of gleaming dark wood, with thinly padded seats upholstered in needle-point. Darcy couldn't see a single comfortable, inflated vinyl air chair.

The living room was just as formal as the dining room, all stiff and polished. A pewter plate and two silver candlesticks decorated the fireplace mantel, with a paperweight that held a lily inside clear glass, and a silver-framed picture of a little boy.

But almost the whole living room was taken up by a freestanding cabinet eight feet tall, five feet wide, and five feet deep. On the floor to one side of the cabinet stood a large control board full of switches and blinking lights; on the other side was a flat, framed video screen. Both were connected to the cabinet by strands of hair-thin, brightly colored wires. The high-tech apparatus looked totally out of place in Mrs. Galloway's living room.

"What is it?" Darcy asked.

Daniel Gutierrez answered her question with a question. "Ever been in virtual reality?"

CHAPTER FOUR

"Sure. I've played cyberspace games at the arcade with my friend Erik," Darcy told Daniel. "Lots of times. We played Century Centaurs, and Wreck Racers, and Sigmoids in Space...."

Daniel's smile was tolerant, as though Darcy were a kindergartner telling him she could tie her shoelaces.

"Uh-huh." He nodded. "Those are all 3-D, interactive, fast action, fun stuff—but—they're totally primitive compared to this." With his fingertips, he tapped the side panel of the cabinet. "This is *real* virtual reality, not a game," he said. "It's VROOM—a virtual-reality room. There's one pretty much like it at the Smithsonian Institution in Washington, only theirs is bigger than mine."

"So what does it do?" Jeff asked.

Daniel answered, "My partner and I spent four years and over two million dollars of investors' money developing this program. She's on the West Coast right now setting up the business out there—we're just starting to pay back our investors. What it does...well, it's a whole big technological-psychological breakthrough. We've combined a virtual room with a neural interface."

"Neural...what?" Darcy asked.

"Neural interface. It means a connection between a human and a computer. In cyberslang it's called neuropatching, or wetware—'wet' referring to the human brain."

"Ugh!" Darcy grunted. A wet brain sounded like something floating in a jar.

"With Rent-A-Memory, our clients get a tiny computer chip implanted—temporarily—in the brain's cortex, which is the memory center. Then their best memories can be programmed right into the virtual-reality equipment. From head to hard drive, with no detour."

Both Darcy and Jeff stared at him blankly. Head? To hard drive?

"You know—like a computer taps into its memory storage to retrieve information? Our interface taps into the client's past to retrieve experiences. In high-resolution digital imagery." Daniel kept throwing out jargon as if they could understand what he was saying. Erik would have, if he'd been there; Erik had loved computers since he was three years old.

"What's the point of all this?" Jeff asked.

"Well, hey! Rent-A-Memory lets people relive the happiest moments of their lives!"

Mrs. Galloway looked down at her hands, folded in her lap, and frowned slightly. Then she gazed intently at Darcy and Jeff. Her eyes were clear blue, not at all faded the way some old people's eyes were.

Jeff wrinkled his forehead as if he were trying to make sense of it. "I still don't get it. Why don't the people just remember their best memories? That seems a lot easier."

"Rent-A-Memory gives you a nearly full-sensory experience." Daniel spread his hands wide. "You go inside the VROOM, and it's like actually living the good times all over again. 3-D visual images. Surround sound. And the smells…flowers, or sea air… It's really great!"

Daniel paused. In a softer voice, he added, "The best part, though, and the main reason for doing this, is that you can interact with the postliving friends and relatives you want to see again."

Postliving? Does he mean dead people? Darcy wondered. Beside her on the tapestry-covered sofa, Mrs. Galloway's fingers were laced so tightly that the knuckles had turned pale.

"Touch is the only sensation we haven't really developed yet," Daniel went on. "We can do breezes with fans, but the clients can't actually touch things inside the memory. I mean—if they touch the images, they don't feel anything. Like, you can't hug anyone." He shrugged as if touch weren't too important. "Other than that, we provide intense lifelike memories, with all the bad stuff edited out."

Jeff said, "Now that I think of it, I saw something about this on Channel 34 news a while back."

"Want to see how it looks inside?" Daniel asked, like a proud parent showing off a new baby. He opened the door of the virtual-reality cabinet to reveal three walls, a ceiling, the inside of the door, and the floor, all completely covered with video-vision screens. "See, the person steps inside here. It's not too roomy, but big enough. Then I close the door and turn on the computer." Daniel touched the control panel. "On the outside of the unit, here, on this large monitor screen," he said, "I can watch everything the person's experiencing inside the cabinet while the program's running. Of course, I only get to watch it in two dimensions. The person inside the cabinet gets full wraparound 3-D. Holographic images; no goggles required."

"Can we see it operate?" Jeff asked.

Daniel looked glum. "That's the problem. I haven't been able to get the darn thing to work since I set it up here the day before yesterday. When I turned it on to check it, the whole program crashed! I'll show you."

As Daniel flipped switches and moved slide controls, the freestanding video screen lit up. But it flashed only jagged lines that made no recognizable picture.

"So where does our dog fit into all this?" Jeff asked.

"Let me tell you what I think." Daniel turned to Darcy and asked, "Could you get your dog to bark for me?"

Darcy gave a little laugh. "I can't just tell Chip to bark. He wouldn't know what I meant. He never barks at all except when he sees a crow."

Mrs. Galloway reached to touch Darcy's arm, but lightly, as though she didn't want to seem too forward. Startled, Darcy turned to look at her. The old woman's voice had a slight catch when she told Darcy, "This is very important to me."

Daniel shuffled his feet; he seemed embarrassed. "Yeah, it sure is important to her," he said. "She cashed in her life insurance policies to pay for it. You've probably figured that it's pricey to get Rent-A-Memory. Like, eight thousand dollars. For one week." His dark eyebrows shot up as he added, "But worth it! Worth every penny!"

Jeff looked startled. Darcy said, "Wow!"

"Plus tax." Mrs. Galloway spoke softly. "The life insurance money doesn't matter—there's no one for me to leave it to anyway. I'm quite alone. It's just—I want so much to relive my happiest memories. But if this young man can't get the machine to work, they'll take it away. I'll lose it all."

"Lose all that money?" Darcy gasped.

Daniel shook his head. "No, not the money. We'll refund that. She'll lose the time on the machine while we try to get it fixed."

"Can't you just extend her time?" Jeff asked.

"Can't. We're booked up more than a year in advance, starting each Wednesday and going to the following Tuesday, fifty-two weeks a year nonstop. People plan their vacations around our schedule. Next Wednesday it goes to the next person on the list, whether I can get it to work here or not."

Mrs. Galloway continued to speak very softly. "I'm eighty-five years old. I don't want to wait another full year to relive my happiest memories. I've already had the computer chip implanted in my brain."

Darcy shuddered at the idea of something being stuck inside a person's brain, but Mrs. Galloway told them, "The computer chip is no bigger than a grain of sand. I don't understand how it works, but they told me to remember the things I want to experience again. The good things in my life. They hooked me up to some kind of machine while I remembered."

Daniel explained, "She didn't need to recall all the details consciously. The scan also picks up what she can only remember subconsciously."

"It gave me a slight headache," Mrs. Galloway said. "But I took aspirin, and it went away." From her pocket she pulled out an aspirin bottle and held it up, turning it around for everyone to see the label. Two rose-colored spots brightened on her cheeks, like the paint on a porcelain doll. What a strange woman, Darcy thought. Why would anyone blush about taking aspirin?

"Wait a minute," Jeff said, shaking his head. "I'm trying to sort this whole thing out. Chip's barking has something to do with the machine malfunctioning—is that what you believe?"

"It's a possibility," Daniel answered. "I don't really know for sure. But three times when your dog barked outside, the program went crazy at that exact same second."

"That's weird!" Darcy exclaimed.

"Not as much as you'd think." Daniel sat down on one of the stiff chairs and faced them. "The right audio frequencies can cause a lot of strange things to happen, like shattering a glass—you've probably heard about that. Another example—a long time ago, when touch-tone telephones were new, a guy over in England could whistle notes in the exact same frequency as the touch tones. He could actually dial a number just by whistling. In fact, that's what they called him—the Whistler." Daniel leaned back. "I could name you a dozen other instances like that."

"So you think our dog...," Jeff began.

"Seems bizarre, I know, but it's not impossible. Three times in a row could be more than coincidence."

Jeff cleared his throat. "Look, I don't know the first thing about frequencies or any of that stuff," he told Mrs. Galloway. "But if there's even a remote chance that our dog is causing the problem, we'll take Chip away. Right this minute. He can stay at Darcy's grandmother's house till next Wednesday."

"Good idea, Dad." Darcy's first impression of Mrs. Galloway, who'd looked like a witch on her deck in the night, had been unfair. Now she wanted to do whatever she could to help the old woman.

"I'll call the manager immediately to clear up the mistake about the dog," Mrs. Galloway told them.

"Wait!" Daniel held out a hand to delay them. "Before you go...do you think you could bring the dog downtown to my lab one day next week?" he asked Darcy. "I'd really like to record his bark on my audio equipment and analyze it with an oscilloscope. I'll even rent a crow, if I have to." Daniel laughed. "Hey, he ought to feel at home with computers. His name's Chip, right?"

Daniel looked so nice when he smiled.... Darcy decided not to tell him Chip was named for a bag of corn curls and not for a computer chip. "Sure I'll bring him, if my mom or dad will drive me. Dogs aren't allowed on the bus." As she bent down to pick up Chip, the doorbell rang.

"Excuse me a moment," Mrs. Galloway murmured, moving down the hall.

When the door opened, Darcy heard a man's voice say, "I need to find your neighbor Jeffrey Kane. Would you know where he is?"

"Why, he happens to be here right now," Mrs. Galloway answered, sounding surprised. As she opened the door wider, Darcy saw two men in dark blue uniforms standing on the stoop. "Animal Control Division," one of them said. "We're here about a dog."

"Wait a minute!" Jeff protested.

"You've made a trip for nothing. We've just now straightened things out," Mrs. Galloway declared. "You're not needed." She tried to close the door, but one of the men leaned against it with his shoulder.

"Orders!" he said, waving a yellow sheet of paper in front of Mrs. Galloway's face. "Pick up a Maltese terrier, it says here. Is that the animal?" He pointed along the hall to where Darcy stood holding Chip.

It'll be okay, Darcy told herself. They just don't know that it's all fixed up. Dad will tell them.

Behind the first man, a second uniformed man held a net and a noose. "Let me get past," he said, nudging the first man aside.

Mrs. Galloway attempted to block the door, declaring, "This is my house, and I do not give you permission to enter it. Go away!"

"Lady, people always try to change their minds about having an animal picked up. But once an order's been recorded in the computer, we carry it out."

Blood began to pound in Darcy's head and tingle in her wrists. Maybe it wouldn't be okay! Her arms locked around Chip and she backed away, pressing herself against the wall, trying to make herself small.

"Look, lady, I don't want to get physical with someone as old as you...," the other dogcatcher said to Mrs. Galloway.

Jeff shouted, "Hey, you guys, hold it right there!" He pushed forward to stand in front of Mrs. Galloway, spreading his arms to protect her. "You heard what the lady said—take off!"

Daniel strode to the door beside Jeff. "What's the matter with you two yahoos?" he demanded. "Didn't your mamas teach you not to talk to an old lady like that!" Rocking forward on the balls of his feet, he seemed suddenly larger.

"Back off, man!" The second animal-control officer wobbled on tiptoe to peer over Jeff's and Daniel's heads. Darcy could see the peak of his cap bobbing. "We got the papers here," he growled, holding them high. "If you all don't stand out of our way, we can go away and come back in fifteen minutes with a police order. Would you like that better?"

Yes! Darcy wanted to scream. In fifteen minutes she and Chip could be far away.

As the argument heated up at the front door, Darcy looked around for an escape path. An open sliding door led from the living room to the deck, but the deck stood twelve feet above ground. The stairway from the living room to the basement was blocked by tall wooden crates marked Rent-A-Memory.

"I told you, this is all a mistake," Mrs. Galloway insisted. "So please leave. Now!"

"Lady, we get paid for every animal we pick up, and we've already made the trip out here to Forest Valley."

Like a trapped bird, Darcy glanced from one cor-
ner of the room to the other, from the fireplace to the
dining area and back again. Her palms grew sweaty and
her hands began to tremble. Stepping as silently as she
could, hoping the grown-ups wouldn't notice what she
was doing, she edged toward the Rent-A-Memory
machine. "Shh," she whispered to Chip, although he
hadn't made a sound.

When no one was watching, she slipped inside the
cabinet, holding Chip. Quietly, moving it an inch at a
time, she began to close the cabinet door behind her.

Just at that moment a crow flew against the screen on
the deck, hitting it. Darcy slammed the VROOM door
shut, but not in time. Chip had seen the crow. He
barked—three short, high yips.

CHAPTER FIVE

D rops of sun-flecked water sprayed all over Darcy. She squeezed her eyes shut as she jerked back from the high wave rushing against her; it splashed her up to her hair, then broke into foamy ripples around her feet. Separate drops of water kept exploding into the colors of the rainbow—too bright! And the roar of surf was too loud!

She should have been soaked to the skin from all that water, but her clothes and sandals felt completely dry. When another wave came toward her, she turned to run and almost bumped into a man who strode through the surf, holding a little girl.

The man wore an odd-looking bathing suit with a top and rib-knit trunks. The little girl's suit—one piece, with a blue sailboat appliqué at the top—sagged from wetness, its straps drooping off her shoulders. Both suits smelled like wet wool.

"Again, Daddy!" the child cried, and the running man swooped her into the crest of a wave. The child sputtered when the ocean drenched them, but she laughed. Shaking water from her curls, she gasped, "Again! Again!"

Then a mist surrounded them, faster than Darcy had ever known a mist to roll in, and she couldn't see anything. Afraid she'd lose her balance in the fog, she reached out for something to hold on to, but she couldn't *feel* anything either. Just as she started to panic, the mist cleared.

Now Darcy was on sand, on a beach, next to a boardwalk. Not far behind the boardwalk stood an enormous hotel, four stories high. White-painted balconies rimmed each story of the building all the way around—it looked like a layered, frosted wedding cake.

Coming toward her on the boardwalk, riding in a large wicker chair with wheels, were the same man and small girl. Seated beside them, a pretty woman circled an arm around the child, who was little enough to stand upright between the two adults. A dark-skinned man pushed the chair from behind; as the chair's rubber tires rolled along the boardwalk, hitting spaces between the boards, they made a thumping noise.

"Stop! Where am I?" Darcy called out, but no one seemed to hear her. She shifted Chip to her left arm and ran toward the moving chair so she could reach out to halt it, but her hand passed right through the woman's sleeve, through her arm, and through the wicker chair too.

"You're not real!" Darcy cried, but they paid no attention. Their clothes were so formal for a vacation at the beach! The man wore a white shirt, a pale necktie, a sweater that buttoned down the front, full-cut trousers, and brown-and-white shoes. The woman and little girl had on stiff, starched cotton dresses with scalloped collars.

"Bump, bump, bump, bump," the woman said to the little girl. "Do you like the ride, Evie? This is the boardwalk at Atlantic City. It's famous!"

"She doesn't know what famous means," the man answered. "Here's a silver dollar, Evie. Give it to this boy who's pushing us."

Boy? What boy? Darcy wondered. The person pushing the chair was a middle-aged man.

"That's too big a tip," the woman whispered. "There's a Depression on, Tom. A quarter would be enough."

The tiny girl turned around to stare solemnly at the dark-skinned, gray-haired man while her parents discussed, in whispers, how much they should pay him. His face expressionless, the man continued to push the chair the entire length of the boardwalk until, once more, everything disappeared in the mist.

"This isn't the real world," Darcy whispered to her

dog. "This is virtual reality. I knew it had to be, but it seemed so real for a minute.... Did you hear me trying to talk to those pretend people?"

She sat down to wait, keeping Chip close beside her, worried about what was going to happen next. All five people outside the Rent-A-Memory cabinet must have heard Chip bark; they would soon unlock the door and drag her out. "We don't have a chance, Chip," she told him. "But I'll fight if they try to take you! I'll scream and kick! You've never bitten anyone before, Chip—this might be a good time to start."

She felt the dog's wet nose against her neck. He began to nibble her hair. "Not *me*, silly dog," she said. "Bite the bad guys." When Chip gnawed her hair that way, he was trying to groom her as if she were another animal, according to her mother. "Stop it! My hair looks fine. Who would care anyway?" Darcy asked. "Just lie down and be still, Chip."

While they waited, Darcy watched the moving images on the floor and walls of the virtual-reality cabinet. It was like being at an ocean resort. Her heels seemed to rest on sand. The air smelled of salt water and seaweed. The sound of the rushing waves was soothing. But the only thing solid, the only thing she could feel, was the dog lying next to her.

A fat lady, holding a toddler around his middle, sat so nearby that if she'd been real, Darcy could have touched her. Other people drifted in and out of the picture, but their faces had no features, and their bodies looked indistinct. Darcy started to lean on her wrist, then snatched it back as it lightly grazed—or seemed to—the shell of a very realistic, upside-down, sand-speckled horseshoe crab.

If she hadn't been so worried about the dogcatchers, the scenes might have interested her. Erik would have given anything to be in this VROOM—he was such a computer-head. He loved to call up screen images and animations and simulations of every kind on his own computer and the ones at school.

"Uh-oh, I feel something," she told Chip. "Maybe they're tugging on the door." But no—it wasn't motion; it was sound she felt, so intense it vibrated the floor and drilled into her head. It started softly, but amplified into such loud pulses that she clapped her hands over her ears as three women sang in harmony, "I'll-ll-ll be with you in a-a-apple-blossom time....I'll-ll-ll be with you...."

A man in uniform brushed past Darcy, but she felt nothing. Beneath his peaked military cap, white gauze covered half his face from his forehead to his chin. Since the bandage kept him from seeing clearly, his steps were hesitant, and he leaned on a cane.

Even with that much of his face hidden, Darcy could tell it was the same man who'd carried the little girl into the waves and who'd sat with the child and the pretty woman in the boardwalk chair. Only now, instead of being on a boardwalk, he was walking on a concrete sidewalk, down a street with small square houses on both sides.

"Daddy's home!" someone shouted. "Daddy, Daddy!" A girl Darcy's age flew down a flight of steps and threw herself into the man's arms. He buried his face against her hair as the woman—the same woman as in Atlantic City—ran to them, and then the man gently pushed away the girl so that he could hug the woman. Darcy realized that the girl also had on some kind of uniform. She wore a yellow neckerchief on a green dress that had bright numbers and emblems sewn on its sleeve.... They were badges! A Girl Scout uniform! An *ancient* Girl Scout uniform. How long ago? Darcy couldn't imagine. Now the man had his arms around both of them, and they were leading him into one of the square houses.

For a moment Darcy became so caught up in the welcome-home scene that she almost forgot the threat to Chip. If it weren't for that, she'd have loved watching these pictures from the past. Yet at the same time, it felt like snooping, like eavesdropping on private lives.

The dogcatchers. That's what she needed to think about, to worry about. What would they do to Chip? "And why aren't they coming after us?" she muttered. The waiting was awful; it made her so tense, she almost wished they would come so the battle could begin. Maybe if she listened at the door, she could hear what was happening in Mrs. Galloway's living room. Standing up, she turned in a circle, searching.

Where *was* the VROOM's door? With her arms stretched stiffly in front of her, Darcy groped through trees and hedges and concrete walls that looked solid but were as weightless as dust motes. Distances were all out of perspective: her shoulder brushed a mailbox while her fingertips touched a telephone pole half a block away. In real life, her reach would have to be sixty feet long to do that! Yet in the image, her arm was the right proportion. The focus was confusing, and there were so many mixed-up, overlapping layers that Darcy felt herself getting dizzy. She decided she'd better sit down and wait until her father came for her.

Around her, colors and shapes rearranged themselves into new and different patterns—sparkling, smearing, then clicking into place. An orchestra was playing somewhere. No, it wasn't an orchestra; it was a funny-looking black phonograph record going around and around on a turntable. The song was one Darcy recognized: Every year, from Halloween to New Year, it played at all the shopping malls. Bing Crosby, singing "White Christmas."

She smelled pine needles and roasting turkey.

"She's using up my memories!" Mrs. Galloway cried. "Please make her stop."

Daniel Gutierrez remained calm. "I'm trying," he said. "Somehow the door got jammed and then the program started up. Bizarre!"

"Move back, will you?" Jeff said angrily to the men

from the Animal Control Division. "You two guys started this whole mess. What are you hanging around for
anyway?"

"We came for a dog, and we're not leaving without a
dog," one of the men said, and the other nodded.

"Then go find the dog that knocks over my garbage
can," Jeff shouted. "Haul that one away."

"Quiet, you guys," Daniel said. "I can't hear myself
think."

"Think! Please think!" Mrs. Galloway begged. "Turn
off the machine. Let *me* get into my life! Look what's
happening." She pointed to the monitor screen, where a
woman in a flowered apron bent over an oven door while
a rosy-faced girl handed her a spoon. "I'm already thir-
teen years old and my mother's basting the Christmas
turkey and I'm missing everything!"

"Can't you just force the cabinet door open?" Jeff
asked Daniel. "Pry it open with a crowbar."

"I'm afraid to. It might mess up the circuits. The
door is controlled electronically—I have to instruct the
computer to open it and close it, but the computer isn't
responding. I don't know why; all the connectors seem
okay."

Patiently, Daniel tapped dials and touched screen
icons while Mrs. Galloway, with tears on her cheeks,
watched the monitor that was outside the cabinet. On
the flat screen, people entered a dining room and took
their places around a table. "Look!" Mrs. Galloway cried,

"there's my uncle Ed. And Aunt Catherine. And my grandma...oh! See her? With the white hair. Everyone says I look like my grandma. She's short, just like me." The dinner guests bowed their heads, and Mrs. Galloway's father—on the screen he was less than half the age Mrs. Galloway was now—led a blessing. Afterward, Mrs. Galloway's mother, flushed and triumphant, carried in the turkey.

"My dear cousin Joanie," Mrs. Galloway wept. "She was my best friend, but she died of leukemia when she was sixteen. See her there—in the blue dress? And my cousin Jim—he's gone now too. They're all gone."

"Please, stop it!" Daniel begged, turning dark, sorrowful eyes on Mrs. Galloway. "I... I keep hearing you, and I need to concentrate on what I'm doing."

"But I want to be in there with them!" she pleaded.

"Ma'am—Evelyn—I'm doing my very best," Daniel promised her. "Honest!"

"Hey! You want that door open? I'll open it for you." The bigger of the two dogcatchers strode across the room and gave the cabinet a mighty kick.

"*Don't!*" Daniel yelled, but before anyone could stop the man, he kicked the cabinet a second time.

A flash of light crackled through the room, bouncing in all the corners, blazing and sparking like sheet lightning, reflecting blue on everyone's face. In an instant it disappeared.

"You freakin' *idiot!*" Daniel yelled. "If you cut off the

power, I don't know what'll happen to that kid inside!"

"Unflap yourself!" the man shot back. "I did you a favor, jerk. Look at the cabinet."

Slowly, silently, the cabinet door swung open, but only an inch or two. Daniel leaped forward to open it all the way.

"Oh, Lord!" he muttered.

"Where's Darcy! Where's my daughter!" Jeff yelled, his voice rising as he stared into the empty VROOM. "What happened? She's gone!"

CHAPTER SIX

Lovingly, carefully, Erik Nagy polished his skateboard with beeswax and a soft T-shirt. The shirt had been washed enough times that it shed very little lint, but Erik bent closely over the solar cells to make sure they were as lint-free as possible. The tiniest bit of dust could reduce the solar panel's efficiency.

He loved the fluorescent green of the board itself. Gold and yellow flecks gleamed inside the graphite fibers the board was made from. He could have bought a red or purple board, but they'd been too much of a color blast, like they were yelling out, "Notice me!" Green was smooth and cool. It had class.

For three times as much money he could have had a hoverboard, if he'd wanted one. He didn't, because hoverboards were slow and hard to steer. Since they never floated more than an inch or two aboveground, they bumped into rocks and curbs. Skateboards were way superior, especially his, Erik thought.

He was alone in the apartment. His parents were at work, and his sister had gone to a summer craft class at the playground. Except for the video vision playing at low volume, the house was quiet.

Erik concentrated so hard on his skateboard that at first he didn't notice when the popular newscaster, Glennie Jordanelle, broke in with a news report. "Glennie here on Channel 34 bringing you an Insta-Cam fast-breaking story. I'm in northeast Baltimore at the home of Mrs. Evelyn Galloway, where twelve-year-old Darcy Kane has disappeared inside a virtual-reality machine."

Erik's head shot up. "Darcy!" He rushed to turn up the volume.

"Earlier this morning," Glennie continued, "Darcy and her dog entered the virtual-reality cabinet that their neighbor, the elderly Mrs. Galloway, had rented to relive her past life. The computerized program accidentally began to run, and engineer Daniel Gutierrez was unable to turn it off. When the door to the cabinet finally opened, Darcy Kane had vanished. Where is she? No one knows!"

On video vision, the camera zoomed to a large, closetlike booth with cables leading up to it and around it. The close-up showed Jeff Kane, on his knees, running his hands over all the inside surfaces of the cabinet.

"There's Mr. Kane!" Eric yelled to the empty room.

"Could you tell our Channel 34 viewers what happened here today, Mr. Gutierrez?" the newswoman asked, pointing a thin microphone toward the engineer.

"Not now," Daniel snapped.

Smoothly, Glennie Jordanelle continued, "During the past hour, Mr. Gutierrez has asked for advice by satellite from experts all over the world. I guess he's taking calls at the moment. Maybe later we can get him to make a statement."

"I'll talk! Let me talk!" An agitated Jeff Kane grabbed the mike. "If anyone out there knows how to bring my daughter back," he begged, "get in touch with us— please! She's been gone for more than an hour. We need help." Jeff tried to say more, but he choked up and couldn't continue.

To cover Jeff's emotion, Glennie announced, "Darcy's mother, travel writer Cynthia Kane, has been on a business trip to Europe. She's now winging her way home and should land at the Baltimore-Washington International Airport within a few hours. Speaking of travels! Darcy Kane's travels—into someone else's past life—are something that's never happened before. So if any of you electronics geniuses out there in Channel 34's viewing area have any ideas how to bring Darcy home, phone us at WBLT-thirty-four hundred. That's W-B-L-T—Baltimore's good-taste channel—three-four-oh-oh.

Or access us online at this e-mail address." At the bottom of the screen appeared the code *info@WBLT-34.com*.

With beeswax, Erik smeared the e-mail address onto the coffee table's glass top. The phone number he could remember, he thought. A telephone handset was connected to Erik's computer; the telephone worked through the computer cable. He'd try both e-mail and phone to see which one got through quicker.

"Access Public InfoNet," he said to his computer. Then he waited. With more than a hundred million Americans trying to log on to the public information network, it was almost always jammed. Erik's father wouldn't let him subscribe to any of the pay-for-use online services; his father said if the public schools were good enough for his kids, the public information network was good enough too. Erik longed to become a serious, dedicated net-head, but he could hardly ever hook up to the infobahn.

Like now. LOGGJAMM, LOGGJAMM, SORRY, USER, PLEASE TRY AGAIN, the computer screen flashed.

Okay, so he'd phone. Erik frowned; he'd forgotten WBLT's phone number. "Call...information," he said into the telephone handset.

"What city?" the telephone asked. At the same time a list of all the cities in Maryland came up on the computer screen.

"Baltimore."

"Go ahead, please."

"WBLT Video Vision, Channel 34."

"Which department?" Even as the automated voice spoke those words through the telephone, a menu titled "WBLT" appeared on the computer screen:

VIDEO VISION PROGRAMMING
EDITORIALS
VIDEO VISION TALK LINE
RADIO TALK LINE
FOCUS INFORMATION LINE
TOURS
WEATHER LINE
PRESIDENT
EXECUTIVE VICE-PRESIDENT
GENERAL MANAGER
ACCOUNTING
ENGINEERING
VIDEO VISION SALES
RADIO SALES

None of those departments looked promising. "More," Erik said.

A new menu came up on the screen:

VIDEO VISION NEWS
RADIO NEWS
MERCHANT'S CLUB
HUMAN RESOURCES

PERSONNEL
PRODUCTION SERVICES
VIDEO DUPLICATION
REQUEST LINE
CONTEST LINE
COMMUNITY OUTREACH
PROMOTION
SPORTS SCORES
TRAFFIC REPORTS
MAIN NUMBER

"Main number," Erik said. Why did they have to list that one last, after all the other choices?

"Attempting connection. Please hold." It was a robotic voice-speak system on the telephone line—Erik could tell by the perfect pronunciation and the tiniest pause between words. Voice-speak voices always sounded flawless.

He wished his computer could talk back like that. Every other computer owner in the whole world, it seemed, had two-way voice-speak—except Erik. He could give his computer spoken commands, but all it could do was answer with alphanumeric messages on the screen. Sometimes, when he made a telephone call through the combined computer-video-phone line, like he was doing now, he pretended his computer could talk back to him, even though it was only the automated telephone voice he heard.

"Why spend a lot of money on a brand-new model if it's gonna be obsolete in a month anyway?" his father always said. "Yours works good enough; be glad you got what you got; I didn't even own a computer when I was your age"—and more of the same, on and on, whenever Erik asked for newer and better equipment.

The telephone voice announced in his ear, "This is WBLT, Channel 34. If you know the extension you are dialing, please enter it now."

Erik's teeth ground together. "If I knew the extension, I wouldn't be waiting to talk to a live person!"

A whole new menu of options came up on the computer screen. "For the business office, speak 'one,'" the voice-speak droned. "For Baltimore's hourly updated weather report, speak 'two.'"

"For crud's sake, hurry up!" Erik yelled at the phone.

"For programming information, speak 'three.' For advertising, speak 'four.' For viewer call-in, speak 'five.' For—"

"Five!" Erik shouted. That cut off the maddening, expressionless electronic voice. A hum, a click, and a new voice-speak stated, "All our viewer call-in lines are busy. Please hold." Soft classical music played in his ear and the screen showed swaying, flowing pastel patterns to keep him calm while he waited. But Erik wasn't calm. He danced with impatience.

Darcy was out there in an electronic dimension somewhere—what was happening to her? He felt pretty sure he knew how to bring her back from wherever she'd gone. Why wouldn't a living human being answer the phone at WBLT? While he was waiting, he decided to try their e-mail again.

"Log on to Public InfoNet," he spoke to his computer. As usual, all he got was a screen full of LOGGJAMM, LOGGJAMM, SORRY, USER, PLEASE TRY AGAIN. At the same instant, the phone line went dead.

"Bat crap!" Erik yelled. Minutes were being lost.

Maybe he should just go to Darcy's neighbor's house. It had to be somewhere on Valley Forest Road, somewhere near Parkville, because that's where the Kanes lived now. So all he had to do was locate Valley Forest Road and then walk from house to house until he found the right place.

He said, "Cancel...InfoNet" to the computer, and then, "Call up...MAPS program. Go to...Parkville, Maryland." After faint whirring, the correct map came up on the screen. "Go to...Valley Forest Road," he instructed, and waited for the screen to zoom onto the street he wanted.

Nothing happened.

Maybe he'd mumbled. Sometimes the voice-command system acted hard-of-hearing. "Go to...Valley... Forest...Road," he repeated, speaking as clearly as he could, one word at a time.

Still nothing. Then, in a box, appeared the message, "Valley Forest Road not found. Do you wish to try again?"

"Yeah." With another voice command, Erik called up a map of a much wider area surrounding Parkville. Still he couldn't find Valley Forest Road—the name didn't trigger a response.

Frustrated, he began speaking nonsense words at the computer just to get it confused. "Gargoyle gym shorts!"

The computer buzzed. "PLEASE...REPEAT."

"Toejam claustrophobia."

Unperturbed, the computer replied, "NOT READING. PLEASE ENTER YOUR COMMAND ON THE KEYBOARD."

"Go to...HEL-ena! You chip freak."

"HELENA...MONTANA?" the computer innocently asked. "HELENA...ARKANSAS? FURTHER INFORMATION REQUIRED."

Why was he wasting time! Standing there flaming a computer that couldn't even sense the heat—how dumb! Stupid to the infinite power! Erik laced his fingers through his coppery red hair to squeeze some sense into his skull.

So what next? he asked himself.

Okay, he answered himself, I'll take a bus to Parkville and find the post office where Mr. Kane works. Even if it's closed for the holiday weekend, there ought to be a maintenance person or guard or somebody still around who could look up where the Kanes live.

"Bus schedule from White Marsh to Parkville," he told the computer. Almost instantly, the screen showed the correct schedule. The next bus to Parkville would leave in twelve minutes, from a stop four blocks away. As the crow would fly. If the crow took a shortcut across Brickyard Road. Brickyard Road, where Dactyls lurked.

Otherwise it meant going at least twice that far to reach the bus stop. Even on his solar-energy-propelled skateboard, he wouldn't make it in time to catch the bus if he went the long way around. In fact, he'd need his solar skateboard to get there on time even if he took the short-cut—because now there were only eleven minutes left.

He groaned. The Dactyls would be hanging out as usual on Brickyard Road; he knew they would. They'd see his skateboard and they'd grind him into the pave-ment the way Jax had ground Darcy's roses, and then they'd take his skateboard away from him. He looked at the schedule again. The next bus after that wouldn't leave for another hour. Too long! He had to get to Darcy!

He turned off his computer and gave it a little pat. Sometimes it made him crazy, but what would he do without it? Then he picked up the skateboard, pressed it against his cheek because he might be about to lose it, and went out to the street.

CHAPTER SEVEN

✹ ✹ ✹

"Quiet!" Daniel bellowed. "I'm talking to a scientist in Switzerland, and I can't even hear her."

The noise level in Mrs. Galloway's living room diminished after Daniel yelled, but only for a minute, and not by much. Then it escalated right back to deafening. A reporter from the *Baltimore Sun* carried on a conversation with a lineman from the power company; rescue squads out of the Providence and Parkville Fire Departments argued over whose boundaries Forest Valley Road lay in; the two dogcatchers were bargaining with someone from the tabloid press; and Jeff Kane shouted because the signal from his wife's wireless communicator on the Super-Transport kept cutting in and out. Glennie Jordanelle stood protectively over her video-camera equipment, warning people not to step on any of it.

"Who is that man!" Mrs. Galloway demanded from the middle of the floor. Since there were quite a lot of men in the room, no one knew which man she meant.

"At my door. That enormous man!" she said.

The enormous man remained in the doorway, which he pretty much filled. "Detective Lieutenant David Murphy," he announced, mostly to Mrs. Galloway. He opened his wallet to show his badge and identification. "May I come in?" he asked politely.

Lieutenant Murphy stood six feet five inches tall, and weighed more than three hundred pounds. His naturally high forehead seemed even higher because his gray hair had thinned; the forehead extended right up into his bald head without any boundary line. His remaining hair had been cropped short and neat around his ears.

"Yes, come in," Mrs. Galloway told him. "Maybe a policeman can help. No one else here seems to know what to do."

"Hi, Murph," Glennie Jordanelle called from across the room.

"Hello, Glennie. I should have figured. You and your camera always beat me to the action." Murph sidled through the crowd to reach her. "How 'bout filling me in on what's happening here?"

"Get away from that cabinet!" Daniel shouted to one of the reporters. "Don't touch anything!" Daniel's tie hung loose around his neck. His once immaculate shirt was now badly rumpled, with wet circles under the arms.

"I'm going to try something else, and I don't want anyone near me, hear?" he ordered. "Stay back!"

"There's nothing wrong with the power lines," an electrician called from the basement. His shout reached them through the stairwell. "All the wiring checks out fine—both the fiber-optic cable and the old copper wire installed when these houses were built."

Lieutenant Murphy bent down so he wouldn't miss a word as Glennie explained the chaos in the living room. When she finished, he pointed to a thin graphite rod she was holding and asked, "What is that? It looks like a conductor's baton."

"It's a new kind of microphone," Glennie answered. "A wireless wand mike. You can point it at anyone across a room, up to twenty feet away, and it'll pick up every word they say. And shut out the crowd noises."

Murph smiled. "The marvels of modern technology—Glennie and her magic wand. Can I talk through that thing?"

"Be my guest. Let me switch it to voice-announce. Hold it straight up so the tip's against your lips."

"Attention!" Murph barked through the mike.

The room suddenly went silent.

Aside to Glennie, Murph murmured, "Hey! This thing really works." Into the mike, he announced, "I'm Detective Lieutenant David S. Murphy of the Baltimore County Police Department. I want all you people to clear this room. Right now! No one is to remain here except

Mrs. Galloway and that computer engineer...." Murph turned to ask Glennie, quietly, "What's the guy's name? Okay, thanks." Through the microphone he said, "Daniel Gutierrez, and Jeff Kane. Everybody else—out of here! If you want to hang around outside, okay, but no one is permitted to come any closer than thirty feet beyond the sidewalk out front."

The reporter from the *Baltimore Sun* protested, "Thirty feet! It's raining out there, Murph."

"Ah, a little rain'll make you grow, Frankie," Murph answered with a lilt in his voice. "Look at me—I just came in from it." Through the mike he ordered sternly, "Everybody out now. Move it!"

No one else cared to challenge the big detective, except Glennie Jordanelle. As the others began to file out through the front door, she asked, "What about me, Murph? You're not gonna shoo me out, are you? Give a poor working girl a break."

Murph chortled. "You, a poor working girl? More people know you than know the mayor of Baltimore, Glennie. All right, you can stay. But kind of hang back till the rest of these people leave, okay?"

In the sudden silence after everyone had gone, Jeff Kane could be heard shouting to his wife, who was somewhere over the Atlantic Ocean. He was using Daniel Gutierrez's wireless communicator—it was just a handset, with no video-image screen. "I can hardly hear you!"

he yelled into Daniel's phone. "What? No one knows. She's just gone! I felt all over the inside of the cabinet but there's no trick door or anything. I went down to the basement, went outside, checked everything."

Jeff looked terrible. His hands were trembling. "How could it be a publicity stunt, Cyn?" he shouted. "This Daniel guy isn't a crook. What? I just know—that's all."

Jeff glanced toward Daniel as if to reassure himself. "He's as freaked out about this as I am. This has never happened before, he told me. Not anywhere, not to anyone." With his free hand, Jeff rubbed his eyes. "Why Darcy? That's what I've been asking myself.... Wait, Cyn, don't cry...."

With a stricken expression, Jeff looked at the wireless phone in his hand. "We got disconnected!" he said. He pulled the neck of his shirt as if he needed more air.

Of the few people remaining in the room, only Glennie Jordanelle appeared perfectly groomed. Not a strand had strayed out of place in her thick black cloud of hair. Her lime green jumpsuit shimmered in the light that came through the glass doors, and made her dark brown skin look even warmer. Her long fingernails had been enameled in exactly the same lime green shade as the suit. While everyone else looked overwrought and overheated, Glennie was the image of a cool, poised professional. "Through with the mike?" she asked Murph, then put it away in a metal carrying case.

Mrs. Galloway collapsed into a wing chair, leaned her head against the cushions, and stretched her feet out in front of her.

Murph inquired, "You all right, ma'am? You look kind of pale. Maybe you need to take some of that aspirin you have in your pocket there."

Mrs. Galloway's paleness disappeared; she flushed. "How did you notice that?" she asked.

"I get paid to notice things," the big man said gently. "It's what I do for a living. Your pocket's hanging open enough that I can see the top of the bottle."

Daniel clapped his hands for silence. "I think I'm getting a signal on the monitor," he said to no one in particular.

"Finally!" Jeff cried. "Does it show Darcy?"

"Lots of people in the picture—a real mob scene— but I can't see Darcy," Daniel answered. "Maybe she's there, but there's too much distortion to tell."

"It's the day the war ended," Mrs. Galloway said softly, calling it "the war" as if there were only one war that deserved the title. On the monitor screen, people were laughing, crying, shouting, and even dancing, but there was no sound. Young men in uniform kissed as many girls as they could reach. A teenage Evelyn—Evie—held up two fingers in a V while her parents hugged and her mother wept. Then the image grew misshapen, looking like a throng of clowns reflected in a carnival mirror.

"It's not good, but at least it's working a little," Daniel

said. "Wait, something else is starting up."

Through the open door of the virtual-reality cabinet, lights flickered. Flashes of color streaked across the cabinet's walls and ceiling and floor, too rapidly to form pictures. One fleeting, wraparound image appeared and immediately disappeared.

"Was Darcy in *that* picture?" Jeff demanded, and at the same moment Mrs. Galloway said, "That was my high school graduation."

"Hold on," Daniel answered. "There's a technical specialist from MIT on the phone; let me take his call for a minute. *Don't anyone touch anything!*"

Everyone watched as the lights in the cabinet blinked rapidly—everyone except Mrs. Galloway. She stood up, quietly walked to the kitchen, and returned holding a broom. "Those people made such a mess in here," she murmured as she began to sweep in short, soft strokes.

On the monitor screen, young Evelyn reached out to receive her diploma, but the picture was spoiled by jagged lines shooting through it. All that showed of the person giving her the diploma was a hand. In the living room, Mrs. Galloway skimmed her broom closer to the cabinet, tsk-tsking about the untidiness as she swept the carpet.

Suddenly, using the broom like a quarterstaff to push Jeff out of the way, and darting faster than any eighty-five-year-old should have been able to, Mrs. Galloway ran into the VROOM and slammed the door behind her.

"Grab that door!" Daniel yelled, dropping his wireless

phone; it hit the floor with a clatter. "Don't let her get in there!"

"She's already in," Murph said.

"Well, get her out!"

Murph asked, "Is there a latch inside the door?"

"No, just an electronic clip."

"Then I think she might have jammed the clip with the broom—I heard a thud right after she went in. Do you want me to kick the door down?"

"*No!* That's the last thing I want! Oh Lord," Daniel groaned, grabbing his forehead. "What next?"

"Whatever you do—find Darcy!" Jeff commanded. He sounded fierce, but he looked frightened.

CHAPTER EIGHT

The manual said that Erik's skateboard could reach a top speed of twenty-five miles an hour, yet the needle on the dial pointed higher, hovering around twenty-eight. "I better slow down," he said half out loud, easing his grip on the handheld trigger throttle. He might be using up too much power. The solar panel was mounted on a ball pivot that turned to catch the sun's rays, but the sky was so cloudy that the pivoting action had stopped.

Balanced on his board, Erik crossed Pulaski Highway, where a truck hauling Maryland crabs narrowly missed hitting him. The driver leaned hard on his horn and gave Erik a nasty hand gesture that reminded him of Dactyls. *Everything* reminded him of Dactyls.

All gangs used hand signals, but the Dactyls took special pride in the ones they threw because "dactyl" meant finger, or toe, or claw. They'd raised hand signing to an art. Erik knew what some of their signs stood for, especially the one where the forefinger and third finger opened and closed like scissors. That was supposed to look like a pterodactyl beak. The Dactyls used it in their oath of brotherhood.

He could read a few of their written symbols, too, that got spray-painted on walls. But now that manufacturers made spray paint easy to wash off with special chemicals, gangs had mostly stopped writing on walls.

The edge of the highway, which Erik finally reached without getting flattened by traffic, marked the boundary of Dactyl territory. He jumped off his skateboard, picked it up by the carrying handle, and began to climb the hill that led to the railroad tracks. Beyond the tracks lay the brickyard.

"Checkpoint," he muttered, as he surveyed Dactyl turf. Throughout the long brickyard—it stretched for a tenth of a mile between the railroad tracks and a paved asphalt road—bricks stood everywhere in stacks three feet square. Each stack contained bricks of a single color—yellow, ivory, red, or brown—and each stack rose solidly like a thick square tower, from four to twelve feet high. They made perfect hiding places for lurking Dactyls.

Erik couldn't ride his skateboard across the brickyard because it had a dirt surface cluttered with broken bricks.

He'd have to make a dash for it, on foot. If he was lucky, maybe he could cross it, get to the paved surface of Brickyard Road, and take off before he met any Dactyls. Maybe they'd all gone away for the Fourth of July weekend with their families. Did Dactyls have families? It was more likely they'd hatched out of rotten eggs.

"Screeeeeee!" He froze when he heard the first Dactyl call—the throaty scream that gang members thought pterodactyls had sounded like, ninety million years ago. "Move!" he ordered himself, because to slow down or stop might mean getting fractured behind a stack of bricks.

Sprinting across the packed earth, carrying his skateboard, he broke out in a sweat. If he could just get to Brickyard Road where the pavement started, his skateboard would easily outrace the gang. Erik still couldn't see any of them, but from the sound of their calls, they were close.

He was running hard when he caught sight of the first Dactyl. Tall and skinny, the boy stood on top of a stack of red bricks, waving his arms as though they were wings. The underside of the sleeves of his black satin jacket had been painted luminescent green, in the shape of pterodactyl wings, a continuation of the wings sewn on the back. The boy's fingers extended like pincers to form a Dactyl hand signal.

"Whoa," Erik muttered, changing direction and almost tripping over a pile of loose bricks. He wasn't a good runner, and the skateboard in his arms made his moves even more awkward. Another Dactyl appeared, on another stack of bricks, and then more of them all around.

"Screeeeeeee!" The primitive calls were thicker now, punctuated by whistles. Everywhere Erik turned, he saw more Dactyls. At all different elevations, depending on the heights of the brick columns they were standing on, Dactyls hovered in their black jackets—at least twenty of them. Realizing that there was no escape, Erik stopped running and stood still. He clutched his skateboard and waited. "This is it," he told himself. "I'm vulture lunch."

The Dactyls didn't come after him, though. They just kept posing on the pillars of bricks, making that screeching Dactyl call, waving their arms and pointing their fingers, while the sky behind them darkened to a hard, shiny gray.

What were they waiting for? Erik knew they could take him any time they wanted to, so why didn't they? He realized they were playing with him: a cat-and-mouse game before they attacked, before they robbed him and beat him.

And then he saw Jax Hawking.

Jax stood on top of the high Baltimore Brick Company sign that could be seen from anywhere on Brickyard Road. He wore no jacket; both his arms were bare to the shoulders, except for the gleaming metal bracers encircling his biceps. He pointed at Erik and smiled with contempt as his lips formed the word, "Wormhole."

Erik *hated* the way Jax always looked at him, as if Erik were several life-forms *lower* than a worm. And he hated that from third grade on, he'd been scared of Jax—running away from him on the playground, giving up without argument the soccer balls and comic-book disks and laser pens and lunch money and everything else Jax demanded. And he hated the way Jax had torn up his papers, and tripped him in the aisles, and hit him in the halls, and called obscene names at him on the streets. But worst of all, he hated Jax's never-ending look of contempt.

Well, Erik was going to get wasted now anyway, no matter what he did. "Jax," he yelled, "you're a jerk! A big, stupid, Jurassic jerk. You hear that? This is me telling you—your brain is extinct! You got that, pebblehead?"

Jax scowled. In a quick, fluid movement, he whipped around and threw a fireball right at Erik's feet. It flared up in multicolored flames two feet high. Erik jumped back—it had hit close, but his clothes weren't on fire.

Fireballs always ignited on impact, but luckily, they burned out after only fifteen seconds. Although they were classified as dangerous illegal fireworks, unless a fireball scored a direct hit, it wouldn't burn a target because the flames shot straight up. Illegal or not, they showed up in Erik's neighborhood every year around the

Fourth of July, and right now, all the Dactyls were pulling handfuls of them out of their jacket pockets.

"Launch!" they yelled. Clockwise, the Dactyls took turns hurling fireballs at Erik, surrounding him with a ring of flames near enough to singe but not to burn. None of the Dactyls laughed; they'd even stopped making dactyl screeches. They were dead silent. So was Erik. Sheaths of orange flame shot up all around him, choking him with the smell of sulfur, stinging his eyes with green and blue vapor from magnesium and copper oxides. It looked and felt like a gaudy nightmare with the sound turned off; there was nothing but the hiss of burning phosphorus.

Suddenly—"Dance!" Jax Hawking ordered Erik from atop his pillar. The rest of the Dactyls took up the chant, yelling, "Dance! Dance! Dance!" The fireballs exploded closer to Erik; he had to leap all around to keep from being burned. A bit of phosphorus landed on his sneaker; he kicked dirt on it and the flame went out.

"Dance!" Jax yelled. "Dance!" the rest of them chanted. How long were they going to keep it up? Erik was getting tired—he didn't know how many more times he could whip around to dodge the rapid fireballs; they were now landing only inches from him. And how much longer could the Dactyls control their throwing arms before one of them misfired and really hit him, setting fire to his clothes? Or was that the plan?

Jax leaped off his perch above the brick sign. Loping

toward Erik with his lithe panther's gait, he cleared the circle of fire. Fingers curved like claws, he reached for Erik and sneered, "Got you now, wormhole."

"Not this time!" Without even thinking, Erik threw himself between those two outstretched arms and head-butted Jax. The top of Erik's skull cracked hard against the underside of Jax's chin. Jax went down.

On the ground, Jax's eyes widened with shock, then slitted into fury as he tasted blood with his tongue. He tried to push himself to his feet, but his bare palms touched the ring of phosphorus smoldering around him, and he yelped in pain. "I'll waste you," he snarled up at Erik. "You're road kill."

The other Dactyls held their fire, not wanting to hit their fallen brother...until Erik started to run. Once he got a few feet away from Jax, the fireball bombardment started again with a vengeance.

Breathing hard, Erik twisted and dodged. He deflected fireballs with his skateboard, but he was losing the battle. When he heard heavy thudding, at first he didn't understand what it meant. But the noise grew louder and louder.

"What kind of place is this?" Darcy asked. "I've never seen anything like it."

From the time the powerful blue flash had knocked her hard against the wall of the Rent-A-Memory cabinet, she'd wandered, dazed, through a strange world.

Geometric patterns changed from squares to loops to stars to spirals, first turning in upon themselves, then bursting out in brilliant, intense rainbows of shifting color. Darcy wondered if she was dreaming, because she seemed to have no body. She felt that she might no longer be a person, but instead might be a ribbon of color that twisted, warped, and spilled itself out through her fingers and toes. "It has to be a dream," she murmured. Only…Chip felt so solid against her, clasped so tightly in her arms. "Don't cry," she told him, because he whimpered and shivered. "If I can feel you shaking, I must be awake."

Gradually a picture began to take shape all around her, of flowers in a huge greenhouse. As if on cue, people moved slowly across the scene, in front of enormous banks of pink, purple, and white hyacinths. Their sweet smell was so thick, Darcy could almost touch it. The scent increased, crowding around her until she choked. "Stop it!" she cried. "I can't breathe!"

The scent didn't go away, but it gradually became bearable. Like an actress on stage, the person she recognized as Evie—who'd been the toddler in Atlantic City, the uniformed Girl Scout, and then the girl who helped her mother baste the Christmas turkey—came into the picture. Now Evie was a young woman, about twenty years old, wearing a navy blue suit with a flounced jacket and a blue hat trimmed in pink. As Evie stopped to stroke the hyacinths with her fingertips, she said, "They're so pretty! Let's come to the flower show every Easter."

The young man she'd spoken to moved closer. Tall and thin, with dark brown eyes and hair the same color, he too was all dressed up in a new-looking suit with wide-cut trousers. "We'll come again if I'm still here next year," he answered as he slipped his arm around her. "I mean, if I don't get drafted and get sent to Korea."

"Then we'll just have to treasure today, Stephen," Evie said. She smiled, until her face began to darken with sadness. And darkened more. It became so shadowed that her features disappeared into a cavernous black void. No face existed between the collar of her blouse and the brim of her hat.

"I hate this!" Darcy cried to Chip. "If this is a dream, it's like a nightmare. I want to get out of here!" And yet, if she could still feel Chip, it meant he was safe with her, at least so far. "No, I don't want to get out of here; I take it back," she said quickly. "It's been a long time since we came in here, Chip, and no one's caught us yet. Only I wish I knew where we were."

An explosion blinded Darcy by its suddenness. Although the blast was only light—light as in daylight or lamplight or candlelight—she could feel it and hear it as if it were living. It felt warm, and sounded like the brass instruments in a symphony. What kind of a mixed-up world was this, she wondered, where sound had a feel to it, and gold light softly melted into the notes of a wedding march?

There came Evie, beautiful young Evie-Evelyn, who drifted down the aisle holding her father's arm. At the altar waited the tall, thin young man with brown eyes, wearing an army uniform.

Words were spoken, words that crept like fingers along Darcy's skin. "Evelyn, do you take this man to be your lawful wedded husband? Stephen, do you take this woman to be your lawful wedded wife?"

Another explosion—of rice! Darcy ducked, because the grains of rice hit her. She felt them lightly touch her before they bounced off. They turned into sparklers shooting starbursts, and skyrockets flowering overhead, twisting around the brass notes of "The Star-Spangled Banner" and "America the Beautiful" and "Yankee Doodle" all spun together. Somehow, Darcy knew that Stephen had gone to war and had come home safely.

"Wow! Incredible! I like it!" she exclaimed, surprised that she felt so happy. Her earlier fear now turned into delight. "Erik would love all this. I wish he could be here." Everything was so beautiful and blissful. Except, as the fireworks faded into vapor, they sounded like thunder, and an odd face seemed to hang in the sky.

CHAPTER NINE

Another fireball hit Erik's sneaker, sending up a little orange flame that sizzled the rubber sole. He kicked away the fireball and frantically scraped his toe in the dirt to put out the flame. Tense, he crouched and waited for the next fireballs to hit. But the barrage slowed as the thudding noise grew louder overhead.

A few of the Dactyls pointed up at the sky, where a police helicopter had come into sight. It swooped low enough to bend the tops of trees with its downdraft. A voice blared from a megaphone, "Stop throwing those fireworks. Immediately!"

A flurry of hand signs rippled from Dactyl to Dactyl as the chopper dropped lower. "We know who you are," the amplified voice blasted. "You guys want to get hauled to juvenile detention again? We know you're Dactyls.

Stop throwing those fireballs, or we'll radio for squad cars."

In the confusion, Jax Hawking scrambled to his feet and ran back toward his gang brothers. The chopper was now so low that its wind ruffled the long wings of Jax's hair. Like a cat, he began to climb the tallest pillar of bricks.

"One, two, three!" the tall, skinny Dactyl yelled, and a dozen arms shot up to throw a dozen fireballs at the chopper. The downdraft from the powerful whirling blades blew the fireballs harmlessly to the ground. One of them, though, had been flung in a high enough trajectory to curve back down on top of the blades before it got spun off.

"That's it," the voice said. "I'm radioing for reinforcements."

Jax had reached the top of the pillar, where he raised his fists and shouted, "We'll be gone before the ground cops get here!" He seemed to have forgotten Erik. "Throw high!" he yelled to the others. "Real high!"

This time, several of the fireballs soared high enough to fall back down onto the rotating blades. When one of them bounced through the open door of the helicopter, the Dactyls shrieked a victory cry, chanting, "Crash the cops! Crash the cops!"

Apparently the fireball did little damage since the microphone was still working. Erik heard the same man's voice, this time speaking to the pilot. "I'm going to drop some Crowd Control," he said. "That'll quiet them till our backup gets here."

Instantly a cloud of white powder drifted down from the chopper. Erik knew about Crowd Control; you did not grow up in a tough Baltimore neighborhood without learning everything the police had in their arsenal, either from hearing about it or from having it used on you. Knowing what would happen and hoping to escape it, he hoisted his skateboard above his head and ran back toward the railroad tracks, where a CSX freight train rumbled along.

Bits of white dust floated down toward him but the skateboard caught most of it. Erik tried to blow away the dust particles before they reached his skin, and at the same time tried not to breathe in. When Crowd Control got inhaled, or when it touched people's skin, it put them to sleep within minutes. A quarter of an hour later, they would wake up with colossal headaches—and usually, with handcuffs on their wrists.

"Hey, not on *me*! I'm the good guy!" Eric hollered as the helicopter dropped more white dust closer to him. He scurried to outrace it; his adrenaline level, already high from the battle with the Dactyls, helped him sprint. When he looked back, the Dactyls were sinking to their knees on the columns of bricks. Some of them dropped to the ground, staggered, and then lay still, curling up to sleep peacefully like babies.

Although his skateboard protected him, Erik couldn't

escape the dust altogether. As he ran toward a moving boxcar with open doors, he felt the first heavy pull of sleepiness.

He struggled against it. If he could only climb into the slowly moving boxcar, no more dust would reach him. At the same time the train would carry him out of range—particles of Crowd Control tended to fall straight down and not drift around. With one last burst of strength, he grabbed the edge of the boxcar, threw in the skateboard, and hauled himself through the door.

Groggy, he realized the train might be traveling to Virginia or Kentucky—that was the direction it was headed. He'd need to jump off before it picked up enough speed that he *couldn't* get out. Had to get to Darcy.

But it would feel so good just to stay there and... sleep. The train wheels clacked rhythmically. Soothing. Like music. Erik stretched out on the hard metal floor. Because the car was empty, it bounced, rattling him around like a stone in an empty bucket, knocking half-shaped thoughts through his head.

Darcy! Gotta get Darcy! Wake up, man! Wake... A hard bump brought him partway to his senses. *Move!* he ordered himself.

In desperation, he threw his skateboard out the door and swung himself out after it. Head over heels he rolled down the railroad embankment. Shaking himself, yawning, too drowsy to care how bruised he'd gotten or how many cinders were stuck in his skin, Erik crawled up the side of a gully. At the top, he settled against a wire cyclone fence and surrendered himself to sleep. The last thing he managed to do was to point the skateboard's solar panel up toward the sun. If there'd been any sun.

Dark clouds rolled overhead. Thunder cracked like steel balls in a giant pinball game. Erik heard nothing. Brush hid him from the view of any passing motorists as he slept, too deeply for dreams.

The first raindrops to hit him were soft and warm. Slumped against the fence, Erik slept on. Lightning exploded above him, and the rain grew harder, pounding the top of his head, but he still slept. Rain as stinging as water from a fire hose splashed on Erik and on the wires of the cyclone fence, hitting the skateboard's solar panel, threatening to douse the solar cells.

"Ow!" Erik said, sleepily, and then "*Ow! Leave me alone, Jax!*" When he opened his heavy-lidded eyes, no Dactyls were there. It was only rain, pelting his head.

"I'm soaked!" he said out loud, stuttering over the words because his tongue felt thick from the effects of Crowd Control. As though it had only wanted to wake him up, the cloudburst tapered off, but the skies kept drizzling.

Erik rubbed his throbbing skull, rumpling his matted red hair with his fingers. He scooped some water from a puddle and sucked it to wash the bitter taste of Crowd Control from his mouth. As he struggled to clear his head, a picture formed in his mind: Jax, on the ground.

Where Erik had knocked him. Erik grinned. For a full minute he sat there grinning about what he'd done to Jax. Then he laughed out loud. "Yes!" he exclaimed, clenching his fist. "Yes!"

He remembered Jax's eyes filling with surprise, and something more. In the brief instant before surprise turned to anger, there'd been another look that came and went so fast, Erik couldn't be positive he'd seen it. Respect. In Jax's eyes, at long last—a small flash of respect for Erik Nagy, the techno-nerd, the cockroach.

They'd fight again; it was inevitable. But if Erik could stand up to Jax a couple more times, and bring that flicker back into his eyes…maybe then they could coexist.

No time to think about that now.

His watch had stopped, probably from being hit when he bailed out of the boxcar—that was bad. His skateboard was dripping wet, with all the white dust washed off it—that was good. For sure he'd missed the bus—that was bad. But the train had carried him about a mile closer to Parkville—that was better than if it had been going in the opposite direction.

Nine miles to go on his skateboard. He checked the battery gauge; it registered only half a charge. Pretty chancy, but he had to try.

"Let's move it. Gotta get to Darcy," he said out loud.

Darcy whirled, because she heard a baby cry. A brand-new baby. There was Evie—Evelyn—in a white nightgown, lying under white sheets on a white metal bed with white roses on the white nightstand, holding out her arms. There stood a starched white nurse with no face, handing Evelyn the tiny baby wrapped in a white blanket. Sitting on the bed, smiling as he leaned over mother and child, was Stephen.

"He's a Galloway, all right," Stephen said. "We'll name him Alan, after my father."

Galloway! It was only then that the realization hit Darcy full force. That pretty young woman was old Mrs. Galloway!—or what she'd once been, years and years ago. They were the same person, even though they didn't look anything alike! Or sound alike, or move alike. Darcy shouldn't have been so surprised—after all, the VROOM was supposed to show Mrs. Galloway's happy memories—but she'd been watching them as though they were episodes on video vision, not thinking about who the people might be. She just hadn't connected to the fact that pretty, young Evie—the little girl, the teenager, the bride—was Mrs. Galloway! How could age change a person so much that you didn't recognize her? Did *everyone* change that much?

Will *I*? she wondered.

In the folds of the white sheet that hung down from the bed, the strange face appeared again, stronger this time. It took form like a plaster mold, pressing forward farther and farther against the sheet. Suddenly a white, eyeless face leaped out at her, and Darcy screamed. "Go away!" she wailed. "I want my mom and dad! I want *out of here!*"

Holding Chip, she started to run. For what seemed like a quarter of a mile, she ran. But even though she felt her feet hitting a surface, she could see nothing solid beneath her, and the light changed colors with every few steps she took. It was like being inside a soap bubble. "I'm dreaming; I'm dreaming," she said over and over again, hoping she was right. But if this was a dream, her arms were getting awfully tired from carrying Chip.

If it wasn't a dream, where were the cabinet walls? Where was the door? Still surrounded by the huge, soft sphere, she sensed someone on the other side trying to break through to her. A hand pushed out at her, then pulled back. That face again! Nose, eye sockets, chin— all outlined in the bubble's thin surface—they leaped toward her, and then recoiled. Darcy shrieked. Hands, knees, the head—they were everywhere around her, and then they were gone, only to reappear, hands grasping at her from all sides through the filmy surface. Trying to get her! "Leave me alone!" she moaned.

Outside the bubble, the arms and knees and head came together to form a silhouette, a human shape. One of the hands reached toward Darcy's face, the fingers stretching the bubble's skin. Closer and closer they came, until they touched her! "Don't!" she screamed, more pan- icked than hurt. As she spun around and stumbled, the other hand groped at her. With a terrible ripping sound like giant fingernails scraping against a wall, both the hands broke through. And then a foot! A Birkenstock sandal!

"Mrs. Galloway!" Darcy screamed.

The old woman looked stunned. "Where are we?" she asked.

"I don't know!" Dropping Chip, Darcy rushed forward to feel the woman's arms and shoulders. This was a real, flesh-and-blood Mrs. Galloway, for sure! Darcy felt the warm, wrinkled skin and firm bones.

"I don't think we're in the cabinet anymore," Mrs. Galloway said. "I went into the VROOM and jammed the door shut, but something strange happened. It felt like I was being...shredded! And then put back together piece by piece. Where could we be?"

A flowing image, all pastel, wafted around the two of them. Softly, a music box tinkled "Frère Jacques"; at every "din, dan, dun," a tiny wooden puppet yawned and threw open its arms.

"Oh look! Stephen bought that toy for our baby Alan," Mrs. Galloway said, her face softening as she watched her young self rock her son in a high-backed rocking chair. "And Stephen made the crib—see the hyacinths painted on its sides? We always said that hyacinths were our special flower." Her eyes widened, then grew bright with wonder. "I'm here!" she breathed. "I'm here at last! Inside my happy memories!"

In the virtual image, the young mother placed the

baby in the crib. He stood up and gnawed the top rail.

"Don't do that, Alan, sweetheart," old Mrs. Galloway crooned to the baby. "He's teething," she explained to Darcy. "That crib railing is just full of his tooth marks."

"How can we get out of here?" Darcy cried.

Looking confused, Mrs. Galloway answered, "Oh, I don't want to leave. I just got here. This is my life—my happy times!"

"But *I* want to leave," Darcy told her. "I'm so scared! Part of it is nice, but most of it isn't." If she could just get out of this nightmarish virtual world, she'd save Chip in some other way. Her parents would know what to do. Darcy wanted them so badly her eyes filled with tears.

"Well, you leave if you want to, dear," Mrs. Galloway said.

"I can't! I don't know how!" Darcy pleaded, but Mrs. Galloway wasn't paying attention.

The old woman knelt on the carpet, as the image of her young self was doing, stacking blocks for the little boy, who was now three years old. Mrs. Galloway's aged, veined hand slid inside the young hand of the image and melted into it. "Oh!" she cried in delight. "Did you see that?" She pulled out her hand and then merged it again, several more times, with the young, smooth hand of the woman she'd once been. She seemed enchanted by it.

Sighing, Darcy sat down, as far back as she could manage so she wouldn't be part of the picture. She felt something underneath her—it was a wooden alphabet block. Not wanting to disturb Mrs. Galloway, Darcy stayed quiet, turning the square wooden block in her fingers. I can actually feel this, she thought. Daniel said no one could feel anything in the VROOM. I guess he was wrong.

A low rumble sounded in the distance. It must have been thunder, because Chip heard it too—he churned his front paws like a windmill, trying to dig under Darcy's legs. Chip hated storms! "It's okay," she assured him. "It's probably only pretend." But she guessed that to a dog, pretend wouldn't matter; thunder was thunder.

The little boy knocked over the stack of blocks and laughed. "Again!" he told his mother. Like a double exposure in a photograph, the body of the real Mrs. Galloway almost blended into the image of the young Mrs. Galloway; their movements nearly matched, but not completely. As their hands raised the tower of blocks for the little boy to knock over, the gnarled fingers separated a bit from the smooth ones, then came back together, but they overshot each other, like two pendulums on a clock slightly out of synch. "Again!" the little boy demanded, squealing with pleasure when the blocks tumbled. "Again!"

The two Mrs. Galloways, young and old together, were too absorbed to notice colors changing in the virtual image. But Darcy noticed. Like cobwebs, shadows had begun to gather in the corners of the rooms. Darcy felt the floor tremble slightly, as though machinery had been turned on somewhere. Old-young Mrs. Galloway read a story to little Alan, who pointed to the pictures on the page.

Another low rumble caused the boy's image to begin fading. "Don't go, Alan!" Mrs. Galloway begged—the old Mrs. Galloway. "Not yet—please! I'm having such a good time!"

The room vibrated; Darcy clambered to her feet, holding tight to Chip. Mrs. Galloway, crying now, stretched out her arms for little Alan, whose image grew smaller until it was gone.

CHAPTER TEN

Darcy was once again inside the iridescent bubble, but with Mrs. Galloway beside her.

"I want to see my son again," Mrs. Galloway said. "Alan was here for such a short time, and then he faded away."

"The pictures come and go," Darcy told her. "It's like—I don't know—like a plastic ball full of water and confetti. You shake it hard and the colors and patterns swirl around all over the inside. Then after a while it settles down, and you see a scene."

"Is it a long wait between scenes?"

"It seems to get longer each time."

"Well, I'm good at waiting. For the past few years I've been waiting for my life to end."

Startled, Darcy glanced toward Mrs. Galloway, who

quickly changed the subject. "You know, that young engineer, Daniel Gutierrez, said I wouldn't be able to feel anything here in the VROOM. But I...I think I did. It seemed that when I was holding Alan, reading to him just a few moments ago, I *almost* felt him."

Darcy was about to say she'd felt the wooden alphabet block too, but Mrs. Galloway added, "That was what I missed most when Alan died. Holding him."

"Your little boy *died*?" Darcy asked.

"Yes. Many years ago."

Although there was no surface to sit on—nothing at all inside the bubble except rainbows of glittering colors—Mrs. Galloway relaxed into a sitting position. Carefully, Darcy sat too, and felt herself supported as if she were on an air chair. When she put Chip down, he turned in a circle a few times and then curled at her feet, settling himself with tiny satisfied sniffs.

"Losing a child is the worst thing that can happen," Mrs. Galloway said. "A part of you dies too, and it doesn't ever come back. Not ever. For two or three years after Alan died, I moved around in a daze. Numb. I hardly answered when people spoke to me, because I just didn't notice them."

Mrs. Galloway's voice trembled a little as she recalled, "Once, on my birthday—it was so strange—my husband Stephen said, 'You're thirty-two years old today.' And I answered, 'No, I'm only thirty.' I became quite angry when Stephen insisted that I was thirty-two. But I really was."

"How could you forget how old you were?" Darcy asked. Two whole years—that was such a long time! The Kanes had moved onto Forest Valley Road only three weeks ago, and that seemed like forever.

"I don't know. I'd been in some dark place where two years slipped away and I never noticed. I kept waiting for Alan to come to me in a dream," Mrs. Galloway went on. "Friends who'd lost loved ones said that was what happened to them—they would dream that the person came to them, and it seemed so real. But Alan never came to me. I hoped he would, because I wanted to give him one last hug. Alan was always such a little hugger! You know, we take things like hugs too much for granted. Until we can't have them anymore."

At that moment, Darcy would have given anything to have her mother hug her. She shivered, remembering the night before, when her mother had come into her bed and Darcy had turned her back and refused to let her mother comfort her. What if something happened to the airplane her mother was on? What if she never got another chance to hug her? She felt a sob rise up and catch in her throat.

"Glennie, would you come up here a minute?" Detective Murphy called from the top of the stairs.

Long-legged Glennie Jordanelle took the stairs two at a time. "What do you need, Murph?" she asked when she reached him.

"I've been looking around up here to see if I could find—I don't know exactly what. Something about Mrs. Galloway. I have a feeling that there's more to this situation than we're seeing on the surface. Detective's intuition. I thought maybe if you searched too...you know, maybe find something that sets off buzzers in your *newshound's* intuition..."

"If I do, will you let me use it in my broadcast?"

Murph raised his eyebrows at her. "No guarantees."

"Well, I'll help you anyway, Murph, 'cause you're such a nice guy for a cop. Where do we start?"

"In here." He pointed to a small room at the side of the stairway. "This seems to be Mrs. Galloway's study. There are boxes full of photos, and news clippings on the desk and the chairs. Daniel told me he used them to put together her memory program."

Murph stayed back until Glennie had entered through the doorway; he was too big to fit in a door frame at the same time as anyone else. "See, the person whose life it is usually doesn't have a clear memory of how they themselves looked—just how other people looked."

"Why's that?" Glennie asked, puzzled.

"Think about it. Through your own eyes, you're always looking out at other people. But you don't see yourself unless you pass in front of a mirror, and even then you only see your image in left-right reverse."

"Oh, yeah. So you want me to sort through these

things to get a sense of Mrs. Galloway?" She picked up a scrapbook that had been left on a chair.

"Uh-huh. We'll both look." Murph moved to Mrs. Galloway's desk.

Glennie sat cross-legged on the floor, reading through the scrapbook from back to front. After a minute, she announced, "She was a schoolteacher. She taught high school English. They had a retirement party for her in 1995." Glennie grew absorbed in the pages, skimming the newspaper clippings on each page before turning to the previous one.

Murph pulled out the desk drawers one at a time. As big as his hands were, his fingers moved delicately through the boxes of writing paper, the pens, the bills with "paid" written on them in Mrs. Galloway's slightly shaky handwriting.

"She pays her bills the old way, by mail," he said. "I searched all over the house and she doesn't even own a personal computer. And no video-vision screen—just a little old nineteen-inch TV she must have bought back in the 1990s."

"Here's an obituary in the scrapbook," Glennie interrupted. "Her husband died at the age of sixty. Cancer."

"Thank God there's a cure for that now," Murph said. He was carefully picking wadded papers out of a wastebasket. As he straightened each page, he looked puzzled, because all of them were blank. "Why would anyone throw away pages with nothing written on them?" he muttered to himself. "Unless they just wanted the waste-basket to seem full."

"Murph, look at this!" Glennie exclaimed. "Oh, how awful! She lost her little boy in a tornado. In Oklahoma."

"Lost him?"

"Literally! He was torn out of her arms. The story's here, dated Oklahoma, 1959."

"A *tornado*!" Murph scrunched his eyes shut. "I'm sure she won't want to relive *that* part of her life." After removing the last crumpled sheet of paper, he came upon layers of tissue paper and lifted them from the wastebasket. "Ah!" he breathed.

"Find something?"

"Looks like aspirin."

"Aspirin?"

"About seventy or eighty tablets—like she dumped out almost a whole bottle. Now, why would she do that?"

Glennie shrugged. "Maybe they were past the date on the bottle—too old to be any good."

"Does aspirin get too old?" Murph asked, but Glennie was once more absorbed in the scrapbook.

The room was silent except for the ticking of a windup clock and the shuffling of papers. As Glennie reached the first and final page of the scrapbook she'd read from back to front, her eyes moistened. "This book starts out with a tiny, beaded identification bracelet—the Galloway baby wore it in the hospital where he was born.

It's taped in here. I guess Mrs. Galloway…" Glennie's voice turned husky and she stopped speaking.

Murph removed folds of recent newspapers from the wastebasket. He peered inside. "Bingo! Pay dirt, maybe," he announced.

"What is it?" Glennie asked, scrambling to her feet.

"Capsules."

"You mean like medicine?"

"Yeah, medicine capsules. But they're empty."

Being suspended inside the bubble had a soothing effect on all three of them: Darcy, Chip, and Mrs. Galloway. Airplanes hardly ever crash, Darcy assured herself. *My mom's probably in Paris now, having lunch in a fancy restaurant. My dad's in Mrs. Galloway's living room, just waiting for Daniel to open the VROOM so they can come and get me.*

Chip rolled over, the way he always did on her bed when he wanted his tummy scratched. Gently, Darcy rubbed his silky fur, working her fingers up into the long hair on his neck beneath his chin. Chip licked her hand.

Chip's doggy kisses were dainty and gentlemanly, never sloppy. His pink tongue curled out just enough, and not too far. He didn't give kisses all that often, but he seemed to know when they were needed.

Darcy breathed slowly, relaxing. Breathed shallowly, becoming *very* relaxed. She forgave her father now for not wanting to give up the house because of Chip.

Grown-ups were like that. No one's going to take my dog away from me, she assured herself. Dad will fix it. It'll all work out.

Beside her, Mrs. Galloway said, "I didn't think it would be like this. I mean—so peaceful. When I first saw the advertisement, it said, 'Relive your happiest memories.' It was a chance to see my loved ones again, especially Alan. I'm the last of my family, you know. Parents, cousins, my husband, my son—they're all gone. I've outlived my usefulness."

She didn't seem old and useless, with her piercing blue eyes and her cheeks flushed pink again. She looked like a woman with a purpose, Darcy thought, someone about to do something important.

"Years ago," Mrs. Galloway went on, "in fact, for most of my life, I believed that when you died you went to heaven, and there you saw all the people you'd loved on earth. But then, a while back, I started to think, What if there is no heaven?"

Softly, Darcy murmured, "I believe in heaven," but Mrs. Galloway didn't seem to hear.

"What if, when you die, that's all there is to it?" the woman asked. "I didn't want to give up the belief that there *is* another side, but I just…stopped…trusting in it. Rent-A-Memory promised to show me the ones I loved, to let me be with them once more, here and now! I talked to many people who'd already experienced Rent-

A-Memory. Reliable people. And they all said it was simply wonderful."

"I've always wondered if dogs go to heaven," Darcy said quietly, more to herself than to Mrs. Galloway.

"If there is a heaven, Darcy. For a long time I haven't been certain. So I decided to hedge my bets, so to speak. For eight thousand dollars I can buy one week's worth of heaven on earth. Guaranteed. Right here, inside this virtual room, I can see my husband and my son again, and tell them I love them."

Suddenly Darcy felt herself falling—she grabbed Chip. A new scene clicked into focus, surrounding them with color and sound and the scent of freshly cut grass. She was sitting next to Mrs. Galloway on a park bench beside a playground; she could feel the slats of the bench beneath her. Looking around, she pointed and said, "There's your little boy."

"I see him!" Mrs. Galloway clasped her hands in delight. "Oh, isn't he beautiful?"

He was. But Darcy thought it was the young Mrs. Galloway, pushing the little boy on a swing, while her eyes sparkled and her face glowed with exertion, who truly looked beautiful.

CHAPTER ELEVEN

"**H**ey, mister, could you help me?"

The silver Lincoln town car had stopped for a red light on Joppa Road, at the edge of Parkville. The front window was down; the driver rested his elbow on its open edge. An expensive car like that was sure to have a state-of-the-art global positioning satellite device on the dashboard, Erik knew; he wanted to ask the man to call up Valley Forest Road and tell him which direction to head in.

"Mister...?"

A look of alarm crossed the man's face. The window spun closed and the car lurched forward right through the red light.

"Hey, I only wanted some directions...," Erik called as the car sped away down the block, its tires squealing.

When he saw himself in the window of a real estate office, he realized why the guy in the silver Lincoln had bolted. Erik looked scruffy enough to scare anyone. His hair was matted down in some places and sticking up in others. His arms were filthy and scratched from the freight train; the knees of his jeans hung in flaps; and the edges of his scorched shoes had bubbled up like fungus. "Yeesh!" he hissed at his reflection. "I look like I crawled out of a septic tank."

Although he tucked in his shirt and tried to smooth his hair, it didn't do much good. Half a block away stood a gas-methanol station; Erik approached it on his skateboard, but stopped near the pumps.

"Excuse me," he called out to the cashier inside. "Hey...excuse me? I'm trying to find a street. I fell down a railroad embankment—that's why I look so gross—but could I please bring up Valley Forest Road on your direction finder? Okay? Can I come in?"

The only employee, a girl in her late teens, sat in the cashier's cage, well protected by the bulletproof Plexiglas curved around it. "Sure, come on in." The words crackled over an amplifying speaker system that needed a tune-up. When Erik entered the room and she got a good look at him, her laughter rang out in staticky, broken-up electronic bursts that made him blush.

"You sure are a mess," she said, laughing again. "But that's a cool skateboard," she added, to take the sting out of her amusement. "The direction finder's right next to you—it's set for Parkville. Just enter the street name, and it'll light up a route for you."

"Thanks." Erik typed "Valley Forest Road," touched the Zoom command—and nothing happened. "It's not working," he told the girl.

"I can't help you," she said. "I'm not allowed to come out of the cage."

He tried it again. No response.

"It's been working up till now," the girl told him.

"I'll enter something else," Erik said. He typed "Parkville Post Office." Instantly the map on the screen enlarged. A red line snaked out of YOU ARE HERE and glided along Joppa Road and down Harford Road to Woodside Avenue. It stopped when it lit up a blinking gold star beside Parkville Post Office.

"You're right—it's working. Thanks for letting me use it." Erik gave her a little wave. She waved back and smiled.

Outside the station, he checked the battery gauge on his skateboard. It showed a tenth of a charge remaining, but when a reading got that low, it wasn't reliable. The battery could be stronger than that. Or weaker. He'd already put nine miles on the skateboard since he'd started this trek. Better conserve what was left. Harford Road went downhill partway, anyway, so he turned off the power and propelled the board with his foot.

The post office turned out to be right where the direction finder said it would be, and showed no observable sign of life. It was closed for the holiday, absolutely and for sure.

Erik stood peering through the glass doors for a long time. The only thing he saw moving inside was the second hand on the wall clock; in fact, the whole street around the post office seemed deserted, except for one human being who appeared as lifeless as the street.

On a bench across Harford Road, in front of a gray cinder-block tavern where a hanging sign boasted CRAB CAKES EVRY NITE—LIVE BAND SAT. NITE, sat an ancient man. Erik couldn't tell whether he was deep in thought or asleep, so he crossed the street to find out.

"I noticed you lookin' through the post office window," the old man said. His eyes were so cloudy that Erik wondered how he could see anything at all. "You need a stamp or somethin'?"

"No, sir," Erik answered. "I need to find a street."

"Maybe I could help," the old man offered.

Erik looked at him doubtfully. He was incredibly old—bony, stooped, shrunken, and wrinkled. Short-cropped snow white hair capped his black face, but the stubble of beard on his chin shone silver. His earlobes hung low—Erik had noticed that on a lot of very old people. The man's chin seemed too long for his face, but his mouth looked firm and determined, although it softened when he smiled.

"You think I'm too old to help? You want to know how old I am? I'm ninety-two. But let me tell you, son, my memory works just fine. You won't find anyone that knows more about the streets around here than I do."

Erik couldn't think what to say, except, "I'm trying to find Valley Forest Road."

"No such place," the man said.

"But—" Erik began.

"You wanna know how I know that, right?" the man interrupted. "See that post office over there? The one where you kept pushin' your face up against the glass?"

Erik nodded.

"I used to work there. For thirty-five years I carried a mailbag all over these streets. Then nine more years in the back, sortin' mail. If I don't know a street, it don't exist. Name's Joe Fitts," the man said, holding out his bony hand for Erik to shake. "Who're you?"

"Erik Nagy."

"Used to be a Nagy family lived over on Cedarside Drive. They any relation to you?"

"I don't think so," Erik said, "but about Valley Forest—"

"I told you—there's no such place. Maybe you're thinkin' of some other street name that starts with 'Valley.' Over in Towson there's a Valley View Road. Might that be the one?"

Erik shook his head.

"There's a Valley Forge Road, but that's near Owings Mills. That ring any bells?"

"No bells, no whistles."

"That's all, then. That's it," Mr. Fitts said. "There's no more streets in this part of Baltimore County that starts with 'Valley.' "

"Are you sure?"

"Son, I am so positive, I could testify before God and Saint Peter."

Erik slumped on the bench beside Mr. Fitts. The name Valley Forest Road stuck in his head as if it had been burned there, but both the old man and the direction finder in the gas-methanol station agreed—they'd come up blank on the name. And Erik hadn't been able to call it up on his own computer map at home either. So it was Erik who had to be wrong, and he didn't know what to do next.

His dry throat begged for an Orange Crush, or anything else cold and wet. He was hungry; at home he'd scarfed down a few peanut butter crackers—that seemed eons ago. But hunger and thirst didn't matter; it was the urgent need to get to Darcy that tore at him. How was he supposed to bring her back when he couldn't even locate the street she lived on?

Beside him, Mr. Fitts said, "Well now, let's try twistin' it around. Over by Carney, there's a Forest Valley Road...."

"*That's it!*" Erik jumped up from the bench. "*It's Forest Valley Road!* I got it backward. Why didn't I think of it? I do that sometimes—get things backward."

When Joe Fitts laughed, his false teeth looked too big for his face. "Got it backward, huh? I have got to tell that

one to the new assistant postmaster. Jeff Kane. He lives
on Forest Valley Road."

"Jeff Kane!" Erik yelled. "It's his house I'm trying to
get to! Or the one next to it."

"Well, then, you'll want to know his house number
too. It's thirty-nine ninety-nine." Joe Fitts rubbed his
withered thighs. "Small world, isn't it? Yessir, I go across
the street to the post office every day to enlighten those
young fellas about the old days, when men like me carried mail in sacks! On our backs! In the kind of weather
no one would even go out in today— hailstones, freezin'
rain, sun so hot the sidewalks melted your shoe soles."

Erik hated to cut off the old man, who looked like he
was settling in for a long conversation. "How do I get to
Forest Valley Road?" he asked.

Mr. Fitts stopped short in the middle of his recollec-
tions. He looked a bit disappointed, but courteously
replied, "Well, son, see this street right here in front of us?
Go right up it"—he pointed left—"north all the way to
Joppa. Right by the methanol station."

"I was already there—fifteen minutes ago!" Erik said,
hitting his forehead with his palm.

"Then west on Joppa to Satyr Hill, and right up to the
top of the hill and you'll be there."

"How far is it?" Erik asked.

"Less'n four miles," Mr. Fitts answered. "Not so far
for a fancy board like you got there. How fast does that
thing go?"

"Twenty-five miles an hour."

"Well, see? No problem. But you better get a move on, son. Look at that sky." The old man squinted overhead, where dark clouds rolled under and above one another ominously. "*Big* storm comin' up. Bigger than what we had already so far today. I knew it when I got up this mornin', because all my bones hurt somethin' fierce—"

"Thanks a lot, Mr. Fitts," Erik interrupted him, switching his skateboard back to solar-battery power. "I really appreciate you helping me like that." Four miles, partly uphill—he ought to be able to make it in twenty minutes, including stops for traffic, even allowing time to search for the neighbor's house. As long as the battery held out. "Maybe we can talk again sometime, Mr. Fitts. I'd like that," Erik said, pressing the trigger throttle. What he needed now was some sun to recharge the unit. But even if the sun had been shining, it was so late in the afternoon that it would have been halfway down the sky, and not too effective for a solar charge. "See you, Mr. Fitts. See you later. Thanks!"

Just as Erik made the turn onto Joppa Road, the storm hit. At the same instant, the battery died.

CHAPTER TWELVE

D etective Murphy spread a sheet of newspaper on the desktop and spilled out the contents of the wastebasket. "Glennie, with all that video-vision equipment you have downstairs, did you bring a personal communicator with a cam-eye lens and a screen?" he asked.

"Uh-huh. Want me to get it?"

"Please." From his shirt pocket Murph pulled a pair of reading glasses, the cheap kind available in discount stores. Moving to the window, he studied one of the empty capsules through a lens of the eyeglasses, which he didn't put on, but just held in his hand.

In less than a minute Glennie came back into the room and asked, "Want this communicator to go on the desk?"

"Yes, please. On the side of the desk. I'm going to call my wife."

"She's a doctor, isn't she?"

"Uh-huh." Murph snapped open the communicator, one the size of a small notebook. He punched numbers into the keyboard and turned on the screen.

"Doctor Murphy's office," a voice said. The screen stayed blank.

"This is Murph. Tell Serena to turn on her video communicator."

"She's with a patient."

"Tell her it's urgent."

A woman's face—high-cheekboned, with thick black lashes behind round eyeglasses—appeared on the communicator screen. "Hi, hon," she said, "can you see me all right? What's up?"

"Serena, take a look at this." Murph held several of the empty capsules directly in front of a round camera's-eye lens in the frame above the screen. "Know what this is?"

Lines furrowed the doctor's brows as she peered closely at a screen in her own office. "I'm seeing the top of the capsule as red and the bottom as robin's egg blue," she said.

"Uh-huh. You got it right."

"Read me all the letters and numbers on the red part."

Murph moved his right hand directly beneath the windowpane, bent over, and stared through the eyeglasses he held in his left hand. "B-I-six-eight," he said.

"It's Mexitil," the doctor told him. "Two-hundred-and-fifty-milligram capsules."

"Dangerous?" Murph asked.

"Not at all. It's for minor heart palpitations. It's quite harmless. Unless…"

"What?"

"Unless you take it in large quantities. Anything can be dangerous if you take too much of it. But if you were going to take a lot of Mexitil, you wouldn't spill it out of the capsules."

Murph turned to Glennie. "Count all those capsule halves," he told her, "and divide by two."

"Thirty-six halves," she told him in a few seconds. "That makes eighteen wholes."

Serena asked, "Is that Glennie Jordanelle from Channel 34?"

"Sure is. Hi, Doc," Glennie said. Moving directly in front of the little cam-eye lens, she waved.

"I hope I get to meet you in person sometime," the doctor said.

"Me too," Glennie answered.

"Let's see," the doctor murmured. "Eighteen of them… that's enough to be fatal. But no one could swallow that much powdery stuff out of the capsules. They'd gag on it. And what would be the point?"

Murph murmured, "What would be the point? What would be…" Suddenly he smacked his high, bald forehead. "*The aspirin bottle!*" he shouted.

Startled, Glennie stared at him.

"Serena," he asked excitedly, "could someone dissolve

that much powder in a little bit of water, say, as much water as would fit into an aspirin bottle?"

"Probably." She peered at him over the screen. "But like I said, what for? It would be a whole lot easier to just take the capsules with a glass of water. Several glasses, if you were trying to take eighteen of them. Which of course would kill you."

"What if you were going somewhere that there was no real water? What if you couldn't carry glasses of water with you where you were going?" he demanded. To Glennie he said, "She had that aspirin bottle in her pocket."

"Maybe… Is she…?" Glennie looked horrified but excited, too, by this dramatic twist in the story. "She's planning to kill herself! She's going in there with her happy memories and never coming back!"

"That's it! Thanks, Serena," Murph said to the camera eye. "I'm going to turn this off now. I might be home late."

Glennie cried out, "The old lady has the kid with her in that machine. What'll happen to Darcy?"

"I don't think she'd do away with herself right in front of a child," Murph answered. "I imagine as long as Darcy's in there with her, she won't attempt it—unless her emotions get too hard for her to handle."

This time when her little boy's image faded, Mrs. Galloway seemed incredibly happy. "No doubt he'll be

back again soon," she said, her face glowing with pleasure.

Darcy waited for the iridescent bubble to surround
them, but it didn't. Instead, the two of them and the dog
were swept into what seemed to be a tunnel. She felt as
though her weight had doubled, the way she always felt
when a roller coaster rushed downhill at tremendous
speed and then shot up again. Chip grew so heavy she
had to drop him.

"Stay right beside me!" she yelled at the dog, afraid
he'd get lost in the kaleidoscope of color that spun like a
pinwheel, with pieces of light flying off every which way.
Around them, a chaos of small bright triangles, shiny as
foil, spattered her like teeth whirling off a circular saw.
There were gleaming flakes of mica, and faceted crystals,
and cubes that quivered like molten ice. They streaked
around Darcy, as plentiful as flung bits of glitter, but
always in geometric shapes.

Darcy wished she had some clue about how virtual
reality worked. She was sorry she hadn't paid more
attention when Erik talked about interfaces and computer-
generated effects, about digital imaging and 3-D render-
ing. When she escaped from this VROOM, she was going
to learn everything she could about it. Erik would teach
her, if they ever got to be friends again.

As she hurtled along the tunnel, the speed and
motion made her head dizzy and her stomach queasy,
especially when they dashed around curves at what

seemed like a hundred miles an hour. This Rent-A-Memory was a wild roller-coaster ride, for sure. Up one minute and down the next. Happy, then sad. Excited, then scared. Right then, she would have expected Mrs. Galloway to be frightened over the crazy gyrations they were going through, but the old woman looked delighted.

"I *felt* him!" she called out over the roar of the rapid motion. "When I picked up Alan from the swing, I felt him! He turned around and *hugged* me!" She laughed out loud. "Daniel said I could repeat the memories I liked best. Daniel! Daniel Gutierrez!" she called out. "Can you hear me out there? I want to do that last one over again, where Alan was four years old."

The bright shapes burst into flashes against the ever-darkening tunnel walls as Mrs. Galloway shouted for Daniel. But in the distance, Darcy could hear, not thunder, but muffled thuds like firecrackers exploding inside tin cans. A rumble turned into the musical crescendo of a huge orchestra; it built and built until a chorus of voices thundered, "Oh-O-O-O-Oklahoma, where the wind comes sweepin' down the plain…"

Beside her, Mrs. Galloway stiffened.

For a huge man, Detective Murphy could move fast. He clambered down the stairs to shout at Daniel, "Get those two people out of that VROOM immediately!"

Angry, Daniel whirled on him. "What do you think I've been trying to do all day, man?" he demanded. "I've finally brought up the picture on the monitor, but I can't get any sound. Look—you can see Darcy and Mrs. Galloway now. And the dog."

"Looks like they're in the path of a big storm," Jeff said.

"A tornado!" Glennie yelled, almost running into Murphy's back as she reached the bottom of the stairs.

Jeff asked, "It's not real, is it?" He looked anxiously from Murph to Glennie and back. "I mean, they can't get hurt in a virtual storm, can they?"

Glennie and Murph exchanged glances, agreeing without words that they wouldn't tell Jeff his daughter was in the company of a suicidal woman, somewhere in an unknown dimension of virtual reality, where they might be about to replay an Oklahoma tornado that had killed the woman's son.

"Nah, they can't feel anything in the virtual world," Daniel said. "It's the real weather outside that worries me. There's an electrical storm headed this way. Hear that thunder? If lightning knocks out the power, we'll be in worse trouble than we're in already."

"*Do something!*" Jeff shouted.

An insistent beeping cut through the rumble of thunder. "Now what!" Daniel grumbled as he picked up his wireless phone. His eyes widened and he crossed the room, pressing the handset against his ear while he covered his other ear with his hand.

"Yes…yes…" A look of intense concentration tightened his facial muscles. "So what should I...?"

Daniel's tense stance made the others turn to watch him. After a moment he clicked off the handset. He took a deep breath. "That was a physicist from the Fermi Institute," he said. "My partner—she's in California right now—she's been making calls to everyone she could think of, and she contacted this guy at Fermi..."

"So...?" Jeff urged.

"He thinks they've—he thinks Darcy and Mrs. Galloway—have been...teleported."

"What the crud does that mean?"

"The transfer of matter. Look, I'm not a particle physicist," Daniel stammered to Jeff. "That guy is one. He thinks their...their bodies separated at the molecular level and moved through time and space over some unknown electromagnetic wavelength."

Murph looked at Glennie, who widened her eyes in bewilderment. Neither of them understood what Daniel was talking about.

"I mean, like...," Daniel tried to explain, "the way they're not in the VROOM, yet I'm still receiving images somehow over an unlicensed and undocumented bandwidth I can't locate on my dials.... You know, all molecules are loosely held together. So are atoms. There are lots of theories about matter being unstable, getting shifted. The guy from Fermi says the whole scientific community is electrified by this news. He says it's all over the Internet."

"Where does he say they've been transported to?" Jeff demanded.

"Teleported. No one knows. Somewhere else in time and space."

"Not Oklahoma, I hope," Glennie murmured to Murph. "Not 1959."

Jeff asked, "So what are you supposed to do?"

"He's contacting physicists all over the world. It's a big breakthrough, he said—this has never happened before. They've got to talk to one another about possibilities. In the meantime, I'm supposed to make sure the power doesn't go out, or we might . . ."

"Might what?"

Daniel swallowed. "Might not ever get them back."

Lightning flashed outside. Unconsciously, all of them turned toward the window and began counting seconds...one, two, three, four...until the crack of thunder came. The storm had moved closer.

"So how long's it going to take for these smart guys to figure out what to do?" Jeff cried, his voice breaking.

Daniel shrugged.

"Oh God!" Jeff lowered his head into his hands. "Help us, please!"

CHAPTER THIRTEEN

The new memory arrived at last, just as the final song lyrics, "Oklahoma, okay!" dropped in pitch and faded into the distance they'd come from. It all ended none too soon for Darcy, who'd been fighting motion sickness through the long passage down the corridor. Chip whimpered at her feet. He looked tired. "Poor baby, you're wondering what's happening, aren't you?" she murmured to him.

They were standing on a wide flat plain that seemed to stretch for miles. Tall grass rippled and began to billow in ever deepening waves of yellow and green as the wind grew stronger. The sound of it built eerily from rustles to gusts to moans.

High overhead—was it really high, or just an illusion? Darcy couldn't be sure because the images had become so lifelike—the sky darkened into gloom that hid the sun.

"Oh, I can see you over there, Mrs. Galloway," Darcy called out. "And there's Alan." Far out on the plain, the young Mrs. Galloway stood leaning into the wind. It loosened her hair from its clips, flattened the hair against her skull in the front and streamed it straight out behind her, as though a rope were pulling it back. Her skirt billowed like a parachute, except where she pressed her son tightly against her body to shield him.

Alan Galloway had grown to be five years old. His hair and eyes were brown like his father's. He clung to his mother's legs, not in fear, but in trust, as the wind snapped branches and stripped bark from trees.

Wind was hitting Darcy too. Hard. Bits of straw blew against her; when one struck her end-first, it stung! She'd heard about straws getting blown through tree trunks during bad storms, but that only happened in the real world.

"I'm surprised that the VROOM could have wind this strong," Darcy said, turning toward the real Mrs. Galloway, who didn't answer. The old woman stood with her head bowed and her hands pressed against her eyes.

"Are you all right?" Darcy asked, but Mrs. Galloway just shook her head, still covering her eyes as the virtual scene zoomed in closer.

"I definitely feel this," Darcy said, grabbing her own long hair as it fluttered out behind her. But abruptly, the wind slowed.

The sudden stillness seemed to frighten the young, virtual Evelyn Galloway more than the wind had. Alan said, "It's not so windy now, Mommy. Can we have our picnic?"

"No! Hurry!" she cried. "We have to run!" She grabbed Alan's hand and pulled him along with her. Darcy could see the small frame house they were running toward. It looked at least a quarter of a mile away across the flat prairie.

Beside Darcy, old Mrs. Galloway cried, "No. No! I told them only my *happiest* memories. This was not supposed to be part of the program. Turn it off, Daniel! Daniel Gutierrez, listen to me! Make this stop!"

Purple clouds rushed toward one another from opposite sides of the heavens. They crashed together into an enormous wall of clouds, which began to rotate.

"What kind of a storm is it supposed to be?" Darcy asked. "I never saw one that looked like that."

In the virtual world, the young mother's face registered panic as a white funnel snaked down from the cloud bank. "Hold tight to me!" she told Alan. "Put your arms around Mommy's neck, and don't let go!" Dropping to the ground, she shielded the boy with her body.

Darcy heard sobbing, but it was real, not sound effects from an image. Old Mrs. Galloway wept, "I can't go through this again. I couldn't bear to live it a second time!" Her hand groped in the pocket of her skirt and brought out an aspirin bottle. Fumbling, she tried to remove the safety cap.

A whirring noise, as if from a hive of giant bees, came toward them. The droning built to a furious roar as the funnel cloud twisted and writhed, growing larger as it came nearer. On the ground, Chip squirmed and tried to scratch his ears with his hind paws. He whined and shook his head hard as if both ears hurt him.

"What's the matter with you, Chip?" Darcy cried. Frantic, the dog began to run around in little circles, howling as he went.

"Chip, come here!" Darcy ran after him, but had a hard time finding him because so much dust was blowing around on the ground, and the sky overhead kept darkening. "Help me, Mrs. Galloway!" she cried. "I'm trying to catch Chip."

Mrs. Galloway seemed not to hear. She held the aspirin bottle closer to her eyes, circling her finger around the lip of the bottle under the cap, feeling for the safety marker.

"Ow!" More and more debris flew at Darcy and hit her; more and more she felt the impact. "Ouch! This feels too real! I could get hurt *bad* in here!" The wind blasted her; Darcy struggled to stay on her feet. It spun her, buffeting her from side to side. It grew more and more violent until it knocked her to her knees, sucking breath from her mouth, pulling her cheeks. Her eyes felt as if they would explode in her head.

And her ears! That had to be what was making Chip act crazy: the awful pressure in the ears.

She saw a white ball of fur rush past and she leaped forward, but missed him. "Chip, you get back here!" she yelled. A tree branch blew toward her; Darcy jumped out of its way. At the same time she cracked her elbow hard against a rock, and yelped, "Ow! That *really* stung!" What was happening? Every time she hit something, or something crashed against her, it hurt worse than the time before!

In the living room, Jeff's voice became hoarse as he shouted, "I think Darcy got hurt! That stuff's supposed to be just pictures, but she was acting like it really hurt her! Why can't you get the sound to come on? I want to hear what she's saying!"

"I don't understand," Daniel said wearily. "Ever since that dogcatcher kicked the door of the cabinet, nothing works like it's supposed to." Thunder crashed, rattling the windows; they could glimpse violent, forked streaks of lightning through the front and back windows of Mrs. Galloway's town house. If the house had had side windows, they'd have noticed lightning there too, since the storm raged on all sides of them.

Murph was yelling into a wall phone, "What do you mean I can't get a backup generator? Yes, I know there's a power outage at Sinai Hospital and I know it's critical, but there has to be a portable generator somewhere in Baltimore County. Sure, I'll hold."

"You're not using my personal phone, are you?"

Daniel shouted. "I need my line clear in case Fermi Institute calls back."

"No, I'm on Mrs. Galloway's wall phone."

A flash of lightning silhouetted a shape in the doorway. Murph turned to see a soaked, bedraggled boy holding a skateboard. "Go away, kid," he ordered. "No one's allowed in here."

"I need to talk to Mr. Kane," Erik said. "I think I know how to get Darcy back."

"We're busy," Murph said, motioning him away. "Just stand out there on the street—we'll call you if we need you.... Yeah?" he shouted into the phone. "How should I know! Contact the power company, or the people that manufacture generators, or whoever. Use your brains— what do you think you're paid for? Okay. Get back to me when you find one. And make it quick!" As he hung up the phone he saw Erik again. "I told you to get out of here, kid. Now, move!"

"No! I'm coming in." Erik straightened his back and strode through the doorway, right past the huge, scowling policeman.

"Erik!" Jeff called out. "What are you doing here? What happened to you? You look like you got run over by a truck!"

"I know I look bad, but I'm not hurt. Mr. Kane, I have an idea about Darcy, but...could I have a towel or something? I had to run three miles in the rain." Glennie handed Erik a wad of tissues, and he mopped his dripping face.

Murph said, "I told that boy to wait outside."

"Let him stay," Jeff answered. "He says he has an idea."

"This *kid* has an idea!" Murph sputtered. "If all those world-class scientists Daniel's been talking to don't have a clue, how's this kid supposed to help? Let me do my job, Jeff. We don't need an extra person in here cluttering up the place. Especially we don't need a kid."

Tempers were beginning to unravel like worn burlap. "Erik is Darcy's best friend. I want him here with me," Jeff demanded. "Stay right here, Erik."

It was Daniel who settled the argument. "Man, I am getting desperate," he said. "That storm scares me to death—and I just lost the picture again." Distorted, unrecognizable color bars jiggled on the monitor in front of him. "If that boy has any ideas, I'm ready to listen."

Crossing to the computer monitor and the keyboard, Erik stopped in front of them with his hands clasped behind his back, as though to assure Daniel that he wouldn't touch anything. His wet clothes stuck to him.

"It came to me when I heard about Darcy on video vision," he said. "A couple of months ago, your Rent-A-Memory was written up in *Popular Electronics*. You program it by date, don't you? I mean, you start with the oldest memory, and then program it for the dates the person wants, year by year, in chronological order?"

"Right," Daniel said.

"So—program it for tomorrow."

"What!"

"Uh...wouldn't that work?" Erik asked, a little unsure of himself because he was telling this experienced programmer, whose picture had been printed in an important magazine, how to handle his program. "I mean, if you programmed it for tomorrow's date, there wouldn't be any data for the computer to read, because tomorrow isn't yet a part of the computer's memory sequencing. So it would pause the whole program. Wouldn't it?"

The young mother clung frantically to her little boy as both of them got picked up and tossed down like rag dolls. A huge uprooted tree rolled toward them, rotating on its roots the way a spinning umbrella might rotate on its spokes. The tornado's noise heightened to the roar of a thousand jet engines blasting off all at once down a runway. Full of dust and whirling twigs, it attacked Darcy's eyes, her ears, her whole body. She winced at the pain. "What *is* this?" she gasped.

Just ahead of her, she saw the young Evelyn Galloway get slammed into the trunk of the rolling tree. The impact knocked her unconscious, and as her arms fell open, the little boy rolled away from her. "Mommy, help me!" Alan screamed. The cyclone, like a breathing demon, moved straight toward him.

"I can't stand any more! This is unbearable. Inhuman!" The words tore out of old Mrs. Galloway's throat in a shriek more tormented than the wind. She covered her eyes with her hands as the little boy in the picture got sucked into the vortex of the funnel cloud.

"No! Alan! Oh no!" It was Darcy who saw it all and screamed because it had been so horrible. And it wasn't over. The funnel cloud still whirled above them, writhing closer to Darcy.

"Chip! Where are you?" Confused over what was real and what was not, Darcy searched frantically for her dog. Wind slapped her, spinning her like an autumn leaf. She caught a glimpse of Chip just as a broken branch blew against the dog's head, knocking him down.

"Chip!" Darcy shrieked. Was he dead? No, that couldn't happen in a virtual storm. With all her might, she forced herself against the wind, trying to reach the dog, who lay limp and still next to a boulder. Dust filled Darcy's eyes, blinding her. Stones and twigs hit her, hard. "Chip!" she screamed, and the funnel cloud came closer, sucking everything into its center, the way it had swallowed Alan. But that had been a virtual memory. Chip was real!

The rim of the cyclone now hung directly above the dog. Its smell overpowered Darcy—the smell of topsoil ripped from the earth, of leaves shredded to bits, of ozone and scorched air from the lightning that flashed overhead. "It's only virtual," she repeated fearfully, fighting the storm. "Like an arcade game." Rent-A-Memory was *supposed* to have strong smells; she knew that because

she'd experienced them. She choked on the dust, unable
to scream as the funnel's vortex began to pull the dog
toward the heart of the tornado. Virtual or not, this game
was getting deadly!

Darcy threw herself across Chip's body, pushing him
as hard as she could against the boulder for protection
from the wind. She searched for his heartbeat and found
it with her fingertips, but it pulsed so fast it frightened
her. The wind ripped her; she felt the back of her jumpsuit flapping against her skin. She groped for a handhold
but couldn't find any; the force of the funnel sucked her
as she clawed frantically in the dirt and broke her fingernails; scraped the ground with her knees until they bled;
tore the toes of her sandals. The cyclone's roar almost
drowned her cries for help as she tried to guard Chip.

Old Mrs. Galloway shuddered when she heard
Darcy's faint screams. Her hand trembled on the aspirin
bottle.

With the last breath of air in her lungs, Darcy gasped,
"Please! Help me!"

"All right, then!" the woman yelled at the storm. She
threw down the bottle; it smashed on the ground.
Bending her arm above her forehead to break the force of
the gusts, Mrs. Galloway battled her way through the
whirling debris toward Darcy, calling, "Hold on, child.
I'm coming. Just hold on."

"Hurry!"

As Mrs. Galloway struggled against the cyclone, her

skirt flapped around her thin legs, and her hair swept straight back just as it had in the real tornado so many years before. Branches flew past her; some hit her, but she plunged ahead, stretching out her hand toward Darcy, who, face down, curled herself around the dog's body. The woman strained to reach them, but couldn't. Every time she came close, wind pushed her backward.

Darcy felt herself lifted an inch or two off the ground toward the mouth of the funnel. "Help me!" she shrieked. "I'm going to die!"

Mrs. Galloway's eyes flashed with defiance. Raising a fist to the storm, she cried out, "You will not steal a child again! I won't let you!"

Her voice was terrible to hear. "You will not! I will not let you!" The vow echoed upward into the funnel cloud. With surprising strength she hurled herself on top of Darcy, pinning her against the rock.

With Mrs. Galloway shielding her, Darcy could breathe again. She gulped air into her empty lungs as the old woman's arms fastened around Darcy and her dog. But their combined weight held them against the ground for no more than a moment before the cyclone dragged on them again.

"It's too hard…! I'm slipping!" Mrs. Galloway cried.

"Wait!" Grasping the lifeless Chip in one arm, Darcy twisted until she could throw her other arm around Mrs. Galloway's neck. "I've got you! Grab my belt." She felt Mrs. Galloway clawing for a hold on her back. The woman's fingers dug into Darcy's flesh as she managed to grasp the belt, but the buckle tore loose. "Hold my arm!" Darcy yelled.

They were blown toward the huge overturned tree where the young Mrs. Galloway lay unconscious. Helpless as leaves in the wind, they struck the trunk with tremendous force.

At the impact, Darcy's grip loosened and Chip flew out of her arms into the storm.

"Chip!" she sobbed, because she could no longer see him. Darcy wanted to pull herself free, wanted to loosen the old woman's grasp so she could search for her dog, wanted to pry away the stiff fingers that bit into her wrist like hooks, but the fear on Mrs. Galloway's face stopped her. Anguished, Darcy twisted one final time toward the funnel cloud, hoping to see a sign of Chip, but there was none. She turned back to tighten her hold on Mrs. Galloway's wrist.

But the storm was stronger than both of them. Slowly, it pulled them apart. Mrs. Galloway's gnarled fingers couldn't clasp Darcy's tightly enough; their nails raked one another's palms as their hands were wrenched loose. Lifted by the whirlwind, the old woman spun into the image of her young self in a nightmarish blending of arms and legs, white hair into dark hair, withered face into smooth face, shocked blue eyes into closed lids.

Everything went dark.

❄ ❄ ❄

"Say a prayer that it works," Daniel said. He started punching code on the keyboard.

"You don't use voice command?" Erik asked.

"Not often. Takes up too much memory." More lightning flared, and this time there was no tick of time between the lightning and the crash of thunder directly overhead. The monitor screen blinked out.

"Uh-oh, the power's off," Daniel said. The room had gone dark. In the luminous reflection from the windows, he turned pale.

Then the lights flickered, and Daniel let out the breath he'd been holding. "I think…it's starting.…" One small dot of light shot across the computer screen almost too quickly to see. Then another. Numbers began to appear. First 8-3-1933 and then 8-4-1933; the digits flashed in bright yellow light on the green screen. They were followed by a string of dates on which nothing had been programmed; the unused dates raced past so rapidly they blurred. Each date of a memory that had already been played flashed yellow, briefly, when it reached the screen: 9-17-1943; 12-25-1944; 8-14-1945; 6-4-1948; 4-10-1950; 12-1-1951; 2-8-1954; 6-21-1955; 3-30-1957; 8-17-1958; 5-20-1959. All the in-between dates spun out so fast that they congealed into a streak of unreadable light.

After 5-20-1959, the yellow-light streak continued for a full, endless minute while the computer searched for information stored under the next 20,498 consecutive days. It displayed a few additional dates from memories not yet played, but mostly the streak glowed uninterrupted. Erik and Daniel stared without moving. The others in the living room didn't understand what was happening, or what was supposed to happen, but they stayed very still too.

At last the screen flashed 7-4-2015: NOT FOUND NOT FOUND NOT FOUND.

Lights quivered on the monitor screen, on and off, then more rapidly on and off.

"What's it doing now?" Jeff cried.

"Shh! Listen!" Daniel whispered. "Do you hear that? The Doppler sound—that's the computer's motor winding down, but it's decelerating slowly, the way it's supposed to."

The room became deathly quiet. The click, when it came, sounded so loud that everyone jumped.

"I think that was the door clip unlatching," Daniel breathed. The door opened an inch, then two. In a graceful arc, the broom fell out and landed with a thwack on the floor.

Daniel grabbed the door and pulled it. Inside the VROOM, Darcy and Mrs. Galloway clung to one another, with the dog between them. Both the old woman and the girl had tear-streaked faces. The dog raised his head and feebly wagged his tail.

CHAPTER FOURTEEN

As Jeff lifted Darcy from the cabinet she sagged against him, and the stubble of his whiskers scraped her forehead. He was real! "Daddy, don't let me go," she wept. Then she saw Erik. "You're here!" she said, not even wondering why.

"Erik saved your life," Jeff told her. "He brought you back to us."

"He did?" She reached out to Erik, but before their hands could touch, sirens wailed on the street outside and a big man told her, "That should be your mother. I sent a police escort to rush her from the airport."

"Mom!" Darcy cried, and suddenly her mother was beside her and the three of them—Jeff and Cynthia and Darcy—were hugging so hard, so flesh-and-bone-crunching tight, that Darcy wanted it never to end. She clung to her mother, feeling the silk of her mother's blouse against her cheek, smelling her perfume and a trace of apricot shampoo, while her father's arms wrapped around both of them. Tears washed paths in the dust on Darcy's face; the tears could have come from Darcy or either of her parents.

Two young, uniformed policemen helped Mrs. Galloway into a chair. "An ambulance is on its way, Murph...I mean, Lieutenant Murphy," one of them said to the big man. "It'll be here in a few minutes."

"Check the dog," Murph said. "Make sure he's not hurt."

"I'd check him if I could catch him," the taller of the two policemen said. "He sure looks like he's healthy. He keeps running around sniffing everything. I think he needs to go out."

"Take him out, then," Murph ordered. "There are other officers out front; have three or four of them form an escort to accompany the dog. Don't lose him, hear! Right now he's just about the most important animal in the world."

"I hear you, Lieutenant."

Cynthia and Jeff fussed over Darcy, touching her, checking her scrapes and bruises. "Are you all right? Is it too hard for you to stand up? Are you in pain?" they asked.

"Not really, Mom. I'm okay, Dad." Her tears had stopped now. She just felt very tired, and very happy to be back inside her own world.

"All the way home on the airplane," her mother murmured, "I kept thinking that nothing mattered except getting you back, Darcy. Not the house, not the job, not anything except us being together again."

"I decided," Jeff said, "that we'll move into the old neighborhood. Right away. Tomorrow. Tonight, if you want to, Darcy!" He stroked her hair. His hands were still trembling.

She reached up to touch his hand and smiled. She'd always known her dad would come through for her. "Thanks, Dad," she said. "But I want to stay here. On Forest Valley Road."

"What?" Both parents looked startled.

"Mrs. Galloway needs me."

"You...you don't like it here," Cynthia stammered.

"Mom, what you said before is true—nothing matters except our family being together," Darcy answered. "But Mrs. Galloway's all alone." Darcy felt closer to Mrs. Galloway than to anyone she'd ever known, except her parents and Erik. It was as though she'd been involved in every part of the woman's life, from babyhood on. Darcy'd met her husband and her son, and knew how she'd looked in a Girl Scout uniform and a wedding gown. That she loved hyacinths and Birkenstocks and was kind to little dogs. That she'd wanted just one final hug from her little boy. And Darcy had been there when it happened, when Alan Galloway hugged his mother for the last time.

"Anyway, Mom," she said, "when school starts I'll make friends again, and I have Erik right now. We'll always be friends."

Daniel Gutierrez slumped in a chair, drained with fatigue, his necktie lying snaked on the floor, his shirt unbuttoned all the way down, and his wireless phone pressed against his ear. Suddenly he sat up straight, at attention. "Yes, sir!" he said. "Absolutely."

He switched off the phone and snapped it shut carefully, almost reverently. "That was the president of the National Academy of Sciences. Calling me from Washington." Daniel sounded awestruck. "He wants to meet with me next week."

"You should have seen your face just then, Daniel. I got it all in here," Glennie told him, tapping the camera with her long fingernails. After the terrible tension of the long day, she started to giggle.

Lieutenant Murphy interrupted. "I want you to quit filming now, Glennie. The ambulance is here."

"No, Murph!" Her giggles stopped abruptly. "Just give me a little while longer. Please?"

"Glennie, be reasonable! I've got a child and an elderly woman that need to be taken to a hospital." Murph's eyebrows creased in a frown; he was pretty tired himself. "Johns Hopkins was alerted that they're coming, including the dog—all three have to be checked to make sure they're not in danger from injuries, or radiation, or whatever. I know you've got a job to do, Glennie, but so have I." Murph took a deep breath. "I'll give you three more minutes, and that's all."

"Three minutes is good, Murph. Thanks. Erik, would you mind coming over here to stand next to Darcy?" Glennie asked, motioning him forward with her mike while she focused her camera with the other hand. "Darcy, turn a little more toward Erik. That's fine."

Into the microphone Glennie said, "Today may go down in history as the first time human beings were teleported into another dimension, exciting scientists all over the world. And twelve-year-old Erik Nagy . . ."

Erik smiled self-consciously and tried to smooth his hair.

"...devised a plan to rescue his friend Darcy Kane from that unknown dimension, when some of the most brilliant scientific minds were unable to do so. Many of these scientists will arrive in Baltimore over the next few weeks to interview Darcy and Evelyn Galloway, trying to discover what actually took place."

Erik leaned over to whisper in Darcy's ear, "Today made history for another reason. I hit Jax Hawking. No more cockroach."

Since Glennie had flicked the wand mike toward Mrs. Galloway, she missed Erik's whisper. And the camera didn't catch Darcy's smile, or her fingers twining into Erik's. Erik's grip was warm and strong in Darcy's hand. She squeezed back. It felt so good for them to be friends again.

"Mrs. Galloway?" Glennie asked. "Would you be willing to go back into the Rent-A-Memory machine?"

Mrs. Galloway's smile was wan. "I think I prefer to wait for heaven. Thank you just the same."

Erik stood in the doorway waving good-bye to Darcy until the flashing red light of the ambulance reached the end of the street. Then he turned toward Mrs. Galloway's living room.

It was as though a big party had ended and all the guests had gone, leaving a mess behind.

"Can I help you clean up?" Erik asked Daniel.

"For sure," Daniel answered. "Just help me disconnect everything in case the power goes weird again. Then I'll drop you off at your house on my way to the airport. My girlfriend, uh, my business partner—actually, she's both—is flying in from the coast to help out." He peered inside the darkened VROOM, shaking his head. "It's going to be wild for the next couple of weeks. Or months. Or maybe years. Teleportation! Wow!"

Erik had been studying all the connector cables on the VROOM and the monitor, so he went right to work taking them apart without asking for instructions.

"Hey, you're good!" Daniel exclaimed. "How'd you like a job?"

"Me?"

"Yeah, in my lab for the rest of the summer. Like I said, it's going to be chaos, with all those hotshot scientists nosing around. I'll pay you an extra dollar—no, make that two bucks an hour *higher* than minimum wage. And I guarantee you'll learn a lot."

"Yes!" Erik said. All that state-of-the-art computer equipment! If Daniel said Erik would learn a lot, it must mean he'd let Erik run the programs. Or maybe even *create* programs! It sounded so good he could hardly believe it. He wished he could tell Darcy right away, but that was impossible—she was on her way to Johns Hopkins Medical Center to get checked.

"You'll be seeing a lot of Darcy too," Daniel told him. "Oh, and can you start tomorrow? I know it's the Fourth of July, but—"

"It's fine! Don't worry about it." Erik had already seen as many fireworks as he needed for one holiday.

"Right now I'm going to seal the Rent-A-Memory cabinet for the night. Tomorrow morning we'll come here and dismantle it to take it to my lab, but before we do, we have to clean it—microscopically," Daniel said. "We'll use special vacuuming tools to pick up any tiny particles that might have been brought back from—wherever Darcy and Mrs. Galloway were."

"Tiny little pieces of cyberstorm," Erik said.

"What? Cyberstorm? Did you make that up? That's good!" Daniel exclaimed. "I can just see it in all the scientific journals."

"Cyberstorm." It did have a nice ring to it. Erik smiled. It was going to be a great summer.